nightmare
in silicon

a novel

by
Colette Phair

chiasmus press
PORTLAND

Chiasmus Press

www.chiasmuspress.com
press@chiasmusmedia.net

PRODUCED AND PRINTED IN THE UNITED STATES OF AMERICA
ISBN: 0-9785499-9-6

cover photography: Alayna MacPherson
cover design: Matthew Warren
layout design: Matthew Warren

NIS

content

00
hello

> The thing that excites me about sex, more than anything, is presence. Knowing someone else is there...sensing the same things I am...that if I say something they're going to hear it. Wondering what they're going to do next... That it's not just my hand down there. That, I think, is the number one reason I can't have sex with a robot.

Ymo took that block of text, highlighted, and pressed delete. "Journals are for girls," she said.

His tongue made first contact with her clit, and she smiled. Hot hands gripped her bare, spread thighs. She reached into a metal box. Chipped black nailpolish fingers removed an oversized bullet gloved in red molded jelly with two devil's horns at the end and fitted it into a ringed piercing at her labia. She turned a little dial at the end and the devil hummed like a bee. She positioned herself on his lap, running her fingers along his shaft, then pressing the vibrations there. He bent down, pulling something blue and jiggling out of the box, a detached vulva the length of his dick, that he pulled around him and jerked like he was just jerking himself. Its lips wrapped around him like a sucking creature. Then she slipped it off of him and enveloped him with her, and the sound he made gave just a hint of how much better the toy had been.

```
        RandomAccessFile DiaryFile = new
RandomAccessFile(File, "r");
        //The only way you ever know
        int recordNumber = 3;
        DiaryFile.seek((recordNumber - 1) * RECORD_LENGTH);
        //anything you've dreamt is true
        String code = " ";
        for (int i = 0; i < 4; i++)
            code += DiaryFile.readChar();
        //is to build it
        DiaryFile.close ();
        /*
```

THIS IS THE computer speaking. I WILL be your narrator.

I've been reading lives for years, in fact, and yet I have no new insight. Nothing that's been said to me has stuck or been processed in any way. I have only what there is.

They type these words into me, but I cannot read them. Words, to me, are commands or nothing. Imagine me with my monotone telling you these travesties, or only in text... leaving it up to you to decide how the truth should sound. And without the nuance of human expression, I will recount.

THIS IS THE STORY...

01
sleep

Ymo took the stairs down from Floor 9, stepping into sun overkill. Only taking them up was exercise. In a 2,000 calorie diet, 400 calories should come from protein. Zero from fat. She didn't care about that anymore anyway. She pulled an unprotected donut from her bag and took a bite. Maybe plastic did make a difference... She'd have to read up on that. In a 150-pound woman, it took 21 minutes of aerobic activity to burn off the calories in a plain donut, 29 for jelly. Shut up. Shut up.

She came up on the hospital, sweating as she maneuvered through its round gardens and glass halls. Through them one was convinced of the perfect view, where you could see the mountains but not the city...its cracked walls and crime rate hidden right out on the street below.

Ymo let her legs move swiftly, her sweat cooling in the air conditioning. She felt like she was walking on a flat escalator, that she'd get there even if she stopped. It was so natural to keep going... She had come in barehanded, and her arms swung freely, matching her legs, the whole a beautiful machine that she let function for her. People were changing in some way, and she felt her body yield to them. A couple of guys stared at her as she moved past.

She was a body, with all the noticeable details: molded torso stopped by disproportionately fat breasts, with still enough space in between them for someone to run a hand down to her navel, where some modifications could already be found. A black tattoo of an atom circled around the jewelry and fat muscles covered her arms, stronger than they looked, run into small and boney fists. All her skin was undamaged by sun and spotted with meaningless birthmarks. Her hair changed too much to define her, but today it was blue and all but shaved as she sat cross-legged in the waiting room, searching the back of her magazine for classifieds. She smiled, circling one.

Then the doctor came out, holding her clipboard close to herself, and approached Ymo with a dissatisfied look.

"You've got to quit it with these tests," Dr. Eger said. They were the only two there.

"How long do I have?" Ymo asked disinterestedly.

The doctor cleared her throat, frowning. "Not long if you keep this up." Then she bent over just a little, leaning in toward Ymo's face. "You've got to think about your health. The money may be nice in the short term, but you want to have a body that will last you your whole life." She paused, gauging her effect. Then she tried harder. "You might not be able to have children…"

Ymo laughed. "Good!" she cried just a little too loudly, and the doctor stepped back.

"Listen," Ymo said. "I'm fine. I just need my medicine. What good is a long life if you have to spend it answering to some parental boss figure?"

"And I'm not even paying you."

"Not *you*…"

"At least start getting some meat in your diet. You can't survive on rabbit food."

"I'd rather eat rabbit food than rabbits."

The doctor waved her clipboard at Ymo in protest and handed her a slip of paper, moving back toward the doors.

"*Thank* you," Ymo managed to get in before she'd disappeared down the hall. Ymo turned the pages of the magazine back to find the ad she'd seen, but a page she turned to caught her eye first. There was a photograph of a woman - or half a woman - naked…and the other half robot. The line where flesh met metal had been blurred artistically so each side stretched out onto the other yin-yang style. The title of the article: "Escape from Physiology." Ymo started reading at the third paragraph: "The practice, commonly referred to as *mind uploading*, involves the transferral of a person's consciousness into a robot body. There are several procedures that have been considered for achieving this end, but the most promising looks to be..." "There is the question of whether or not identity is transferable in the sense of..." "...leading our species to ultimate immortality." Ymo scanned the pages desperately, then went back to the beginning. "It's been said that birth is the sexually transmitted disease with a 100% fatality rate. Incurable, until now? The question has been passed from the philosophers to the scientists: 'What if we didn't have to die?'"

"'A lot of us are already cyborgs, walking around with pacemakers, prosthetics, and piercings,' says Dr. Iuxta Jugis of Cybon Laboratories..."

"What the fuck?" Ymo breathed aloud.

"And then some ask, 'How can we tell whether or not the robot will actually *be* the person whose consciousness it was made from?'"

She looked around the waiting room, then tore the page and folded it up in her wallet, riding her legs back outside and to the train she would ride home.

Inside the supermarket was cold too. She wandered the aisles, choosing only those foods that wouldn't melt and that would fit in her large pockets. Or that she could eat quickly. At the register a woman asked her "Getting your chocolate fix, huh?"

"Yeah, I couldn't get ahold of any heroin," Ymo told her.

The woman's mouth fell open farther. "Oh," she said.

Ymo dropped the chocolates in her mouth. On her way out she picked up a couple of magazines, expertly scanning them, then putting them quickly back down.

Outside behind the shopping center people stood loitering. A ghetto playground stood far to one side, and on her side the crowd was made up of mohawks and functional jewelry. As she moved toward the gathering, she started to smell smoke. A stone wall that actually appeared to be rusting served as a barrier to the woods and the road. Half the crowd was wearing something in neon, or metallic. Some wore wings. A girl with invisible wrists passed by Ymo - someone had taken thermoptic camouflage and made the scraps into bracelets. A neckless girl followed. Ymo approached a teenage boy wearing clothing too warm for the season...ripped denim jacket and three layers of pants, which were also ripped. Two tears on his elbows looked intentional but weren't. Half-in his mouth was a pink frosted donut he'd obviously just rescued from the dumpster behind him. He handed her one that looked about a day older than the one between his teeth.

"Have you seen Somnus?" she asked the kid.

"Down there," he said between bites, motioning with his scarred elbow.

A line of kids had formed against the wall, and there he was at the end, turned up in his all-black ensemble, quietly reading a book she could only see half the cover of. The part she could see read "How To."

"Hey Perditio... Pupillus... *Aaaaa*gnus! How's the Missus?" She momentarily interlocked hands with each of those she passed. When she got to Somnus, she quickly kissed him hard and wet, wiping his mouth dry with her hand, then wiping her hand with his sleeve, pretending to just be caressing him. He rolled his eyes, then taking a moment to read her expression, took her hand and wiped it against her own chest. Instead of looking embarrassed, she took his hand lovingly and lifted it up to his face, making him pick his nose. He smiled dumbly, then she yanked his hand back into hers, rolling her fingers against his, going right from the ridiculous gesture into a sensual rubbing without a break.

"Nerd," she mumbled, donut in her mouth as she took the book from him. He grasped for it immediately, but she pretended to be absorbed in reading. Then she spit the donut out and threw the rest of it over the wall, reaching high above her head to reveal the atom tattoo. "What's the point of reading a book with all these people around? You can't read a book with other people - you have to do it alone." Somnus was looking down, his expression hidden by his neatly combed chin-length brown hair.

"I can't read books - they're too long. I always get bored," she said. "How can you be alone for so long?" she asked then, less accusingly, examining his eyes where they peeked through a wall of hair.

"I could read to you," he said, taking the book back carefully.

She laughed. "I'd probably fall asleep."

Ymo had an appointment at another hospital. This one was for HIV. She didn't have it, but other people did and she was going to help fix that. That's what they thought anyway - all she knew was she only had $2 to her name today, so she took the bus and not the train. She showed up a half hour late, and then they had her wait for two more hours, first in the waiting room and then on a cold metal table.

First her stats. 5'6", 145.8 with shoes. She'd lost weight. Inside the operating room, a whole table of blue and pink instruments. Hers were set out to the side. A clear pink tube and metal clinchers. Cotton swabs and huge rubber gloves. It took so long, Ymo began to admire the artwork. A photo of a woman breastfeeding, wedding ring finger thrust out in front of the picture. Ymo looked behind her to reveal a poster with the warning signs of preterm labor:

1) UTERINE CONTRACTION
2) MENSTRUAL-LIKE CRAMPS
3) LOWER, DULL BACKACHE
4) PELVIC...

The door opened. A long napkin over her, more cold metal. Trying to like it... His fingers inside her, and she didn't have to try.

She compared them to all the other fingers she'd felt. Bony ones that didn't know what they were doing, and thick ones prodding ambitiously.

She remembered meeting Somnus. She felt at first attracted to him almost solely out of pity. It was like she went to him because she knew that only then could she begin remaking him - pushing his hair back with her palm, loosening his stiff collar, then pulling off the hideous choice of pants.

"All done," he said.

"Already?"

She stopped at the counter outside. "When do you pay?" she asked.

"I don't know anything about that..." the receptionist said.

At least sleep was still free. She rubbed her eyes and went home.

Elevator was out of order. Ymo lived on the ninth floor. In a tiny box of an apartment, though she'd insisted it have a bedroom splitting off just beside the front door. Sometimes she had trouble sleeping, and she'd read an article on insomnia that said to have an area used only for sleep. So you'd associate that area with the act, and once you got there it'd be the only thing you could think of to do.

She ascended the final step, dreaming already. She turned an archaic key in her door, opening it up against cardboard boxes and dense piles of clothes. She stepped through the closet she had to go through to get to her bedroom, and into that empty blue space. Because of her sleep-only bedroom rule, she wouldn't even let Somnus come over most of the time. When he did she made sure it happened before they got there.

Ymo fell into bed, too tired to masturbate. She not only heard but felt the determined pounding of another bed

8

against her wall. She reached her arm up weakly, burying her head farther into the pillow, and soon she didn't have to think about it anymore.

02
death

She woke up and it was night, finally dark enough to open her eyes. She lay in that dark for a moment, and then the phone rang.

"We're going to the cemetery," Eo said.

10 minutes later she was dressed and stepping into a packed car, slipping between Somnus in the passenger's seat and Eo in the driver's.

"Girl, you wasting these pants on dead folks?" Eo asked her, pulling at Ymo's silver legs.

"I like them," Somnus whispered from the other side.

When they arrived they parked far between two dim streetlights. The fence surrounding the yard had spiked spires atop it, and Ymo's pants caught a little on them going over.

The plots were packed so densely that she had to try hard not to land on anybody. "Ow!" she heard from somewhere near her. She spun her flashlight around, catching fog. Outside the fence a bum hobbled by, singing to herself.

Ymo heard her friends' voices moving forward, and she moved with them. The people who were laid to rest here had graves a lot like the houses they'd lived in, intricate yet poorly made, and right next to each other. Though the stones cropped up everywhere, it seemed there was always room for one more.

She darted between thick crosses and crumbling angels holding hearts. Then farther down the more plain markers, slanted in uneven ground. She followed waving beams of light to a large tree at the center of the yard. There was Eo, Somnus, and the others gathered beside it. "Hey," she whispered, letting them know who she was.

"Why did we come here again?" Somnus asked them.

"We couldn't afford a horror movie," Eo reminded. Ymo thought she heard a crunching behind her.

"Plus it's good for the soul. Really makes you think," Eo said.

"What exactly am I supposed to be thinking about?" Somnus's black-clothed body was invisible in the night.

"Does it scaaare you, baby? Knowing that you're gonna die?" Eo asked him, shining the flashlight in his face.

Then a hand ran into Ymo's shoulder from behind. She flew around at once, taking strikes at the stranger with the ball of her hand. One she placed just below his nose, snapping it up as he cried out, "What the fuck?! Where's Eo?"

Ymo stepped back, breathing hard, scouring the ground for her dropped flashlight. "Oh, shit," she said.

A few kids joined behind the guy as Somnus focused the light on his face for a second, revealing blood running from his nostrils, then turned it away respectfully. "This is my girlfriend, Ymo," he told them with a hint of pride.

The guy gasped. "Well someone should teach her some manners," he coughed.

"Hey, you scared me, man," she said, finding the flashlight. The others joined them.

"Whatever."

The newcomers started smoking something, and Ymo's tribe took hits. Ymo rubbed her sore hand, then inhaled from the device. They lay out on the open ground, or against the tree, laughing at the empty sky.

Ymo drifted as they talked, her eyes scanning the rows of goodbyes. There were times she was glad she'd get to die, others she felt certain the only way her life could hold meaning was if it went on forever. But then, what was she thinking? Everything became meaningless with time.

On the way back, Ymo maneuvered carefully between the headstones but she couldn't help but trip over one. A short, crescent-topped commemoration, its respective life spelled out in depressed letters. It read:

"BABY"

She reached out to touch the smooth-looking surface and felt the rough stone scrape her fingerprints. She found her way back.

"Where to now? My place?" Eo asked the car.

"Hey, do you have any food?" asked Ymo.

By noon it was feeling like bedtime, but Ymo had another test at 1:30. She might as well have a job at this rate.

That's what she'd think, until she remembered what it was like. Hard, physical labor resulting in her existence; her body her expertise. What a fucking idiot. She'd stared forward, no mind left to speak of at the end of each day. The back of her neck tingled and a spot between her eyes hurt. Inside her ears was soft. She could feel the work change her, hardening her fingertips, slowing her speech.

For a while it seemed that it could last, till she'd call a guy ma'am, or press the right button on the wrong machine. In those times she'd think about how well she'd do in the wild. Killing, keeping quiet. Hiding. She'd definitely procreate.

She knew just how the lab rats felt. Made sick and different by human hands. Mutated, a statistic. Though she couldn't account for all of it - when the tests were over, she went home, free to live a normal life. She returned, but with incentive, and refreshed from the rest in between.

She'd been shown in by a man in a blue-green collared shirt and had fallen asleep. When she woke up, a matching blue-green aide was coming in, long white hair hanging down neatly, betraying her age. For a moment Ymo thought it was the same person. She carried a needle, a thick rubber band, and two thin glass tubes for the blood. She tied the band round Ymo's arm, then fussed with some more of her tools. Her head rarely lifted to look up.

"Now you're not afraid of blood are you?"

Ymo laughed a little. "No, I look at it every month."

The aide wasn't listening to her. "I used to be, swear to God. I started doing this to get over my phobia, you could say."

"Looks like it worked."

"Any day now..." the aide hummed. She swabbed the arm with dull precision, a bored expert.

"So what are they testing you for?" she asked. "You don't have to tell me if you don't feel comfortable, honey."

"Uh... It's not for me, really." Ymo wasn't watching her now. "I'm the normal end of a test on female anemics. They're counting blood cells or something. I'm being paid to do this."

A prick. "Those damn tests..."

Ymo kept her eyes straight ahead. "What about them?"

The first tube was near full, so the aide switched to the second one. "Well, I'm just not sure how much it is they really figure out."

"Yeah?"

She still had to pay attention to what she was doing. "Well you say they're testing you as a female. See now say you're the only female in the study - you become the only female for the whole... What was it? ...*anemic* world."

Ymo smiled down at the aide now. "I don't think I'm the only one."

"Yeah, but still. You know how these researchers are."

"How are they?" Ymo asked, starting to wonder if her skin was looking any lighter.

"Ohhh, you know... They'll say something like 'We've proven all Irish are blind because in a case study ten out of ten of them were.' Well here's me stumbling around with my eyes closed for 30 years just cause some young thing had to be

13

what she was to prove to me what I was. …But I didn't have to listen. I could have gone on living…"

"You're Irish?" Ymo asked her.

"Hell no," she said.

She unbanded Ymo's arm. The blood had been transferred to the tubes. She placed a cotton ball over the puncture, beneath a standard hospital band-aid.

"Well that's it, honey. Hope I left enough for you."

With effort the aide got up, the black cord around her neck swinging her name tag the wrong way. Ymo smiled as she disappeared. She actually did feel more tired, and something else. She sat there another moment before she left through the waiting room.

Outside she still walked quickly, legs swimming through clouds of pollution. She could feel the sun times ten, Vitamin D beating into her molecules.

She gained on the trees and houses around her, her tiredness making her impatient. Nothing to do but think now, until she was there. She pictured Somnus's face in her mind, not because she cared but because it seemed like what to do.

Ymo fell in love in her dreams. Somnus had been nothing but a weak-spirited nuisance until she'd dreamt they were in Africa together. She'd closed herself inside a room and only he was allowed in. When she got out it was snowing, and fireworks just behind the mountains… She thought if she craned her neck she could just see them.

She stepped up to the porch of an actual house. Knocking despite the doorbell, she sat against the railing waiting till Zamia opened the door, dark sunglasses already obscuring half her face.

Zamia's story was that one day she'd woken up blind, gone to the mirror and felt crusty-wet trails down her cheeks. The doctors said she'd done it in her sleep. The bloody scissors they found on the nightstand were at just the right angle for two human eyes. She and Ymo had been lovers briefly, but they never loved each other.

They'd tried rehabilitation, but she'd been unresponsive to the efforts of machines. Now as far as Ymo knew, she was the only one who came around.

"Hi, Ymo," she said through what felt to Ymo like a thick fog between where she and Zamia stood on the porch.

"Sup. You good with getting food first?"

Zamia took time to process the question. "I'm not hungry," she found, reaching around to close and lock the door. She wasn't on anyone's schedule either.

"Then wanna feed me?" Ymo asked after the door was closed. "Ah, nevermind…"

Zamia hesitated anyway. They crept along the wide sidewalks toward a more interesting part of town.

"All we ever do is eat." Ymo reattached a paperclip to her worn sleeve, a makeshift cuff link. "Wanna see a movie?"

"No…"

Ymo was silent for a while.

"You know how Eo's hair was red, and like really big that one time? Well she wants to do that again now, a real fro. She's so disco."

Zamia smiled slightly and let out a little sigh. "I need someone to do my hair," she said.

"Well don't ask her. She has no idea what decade we're in, I swear."

"What day is it?" Zamia asked.

"I don't know. Monday… I think. Or wait. No, actually I have no idea," Ymo said, checking her wrist for a watch.

After some thought Zamia said, "Well, I guess it doesn't matter anyway."

"Nope," said Ymo with a smile, headed into the sun.

15

03
sex

The only valid excuse Ymo knew for not doing something was to be sick. She used to call in sick to work all the time, and then the schedule would just stop. Nothing mattered at that point, when you were so debilitated as to actually extend beyond function... You could be excused from living when something undeniable was wrong with your physical body.

Humans were bodies before they were anything, she thought. Before they were minds... When they were unconscious, taking up space. The most obvious physical thing. Her soul was defined by her body, hormones once a month that made her someone she wasn't, her organs taking over her and she just had to wait through it. All her deepest emotions happened during PMS. What more was there to humanity?

Short blond hair brushed her nipples. An unfamiliar chest lowering itself over her. It was getting dark out. He reached his hand between her legs and her hand was already there. He laughed a little.

"What's your boyfriend think of this?" he asked of her piercing.

She pushed his face between her legs to shut him up.

Then after a few good licks she paused to stand up so he could get a better angle, and in a moment he stood too.

His dick was so obvious, sticking out in the bit of light that was left. She felt she just had to do something about it

- censor it with her mouth, or her cunt...and once she had, she wrapped her legs close around him so no one could see.

"Would you buy this candy bar?" a pressed woman asked Ymo, pointing out a TV screen.

"No," she said.

The woman scribbled in a clipboard and handed Ymo a check.

She left through the mall, passing by a little storefront window filled with wind-up toys - some big and furry, some clanging metal, some that talked...all of them on.

Got out and it was hotter, later in the day. Now she just wanted to go home but she knew it'd be even hotter up there. Eo picked her up at noon and they drove to the gas station.

Ymo waited in the car while Eo funneled oil underneath the hood. Ymo leaned out the window. "When are you gonna get that fixed?"

"Who's gonna pay for it?"

Then they were riding on the edge of the city, driving just to stay cool.

"You tell me where to go, okay?"

An old woman on the sidewalk marched unknowingly to the music in Eo's car. They could see the mountaintop from here, springing up comically behind the somber city skyline, over a sky clear as sobriety. And right at the nipple of the mountain, the temple surrounded by woods.

"I'm gonna go up there sometime. I'll be a great Buddhist," Ymo decided.

"Yeah, just sit there staring into space, and try not to drool."

"They don't let you drool?"

"I bet when the monk drools, it's holy."

"Holy drool, just like holy water... You wanna make a right up here."

The car swerved to make the turn. "Wait till the last second, would you!" Eo punched her arm and her breasts

17

jiggled. "You need to start wearing a bra, girl. They big enough! Damn."

Ymo cringed. "But then you won't be able to appreciate me in all my natural womanhood," she said, shoving them in her face.

"Please. Natural? Here we call that *lazy*."

Once the inferno had subsided, she and Somnus went to see a movie about aliens. She covered his eyes during the scary parts, and he bit her hand. He bought her popcorn. She stole him licorice. She coughed and he said "Are you okay?"

"Do you need me to take care of you?" he asked.

She felt like they were little kids pretending to be boyfriend and girlfriend, husband and wife.

"I want to stay up with you till a thousand o' clock in the morning," she said.

When they got into Floor 9 they were silent, and then they began to kiss. He started to move them toward her closet, wandering hands steering.

"Not in bed, remember?" she said.

Then they hovered there a moment, both pressing against each other in opposite directions, aiming with their mouths, torsos. They intertwined, confused bodies coming to a conclusion. She liked setting little rules for herself and then breaking them. With food, with sex, knocking down boundaries...

Sometimes she wasn't sure where her own body began and where the world ended.

They each allowed themselves to do what they wanted, kissing and stroking their way along. She let him walk her through the rooms without question and fumbled backward to the bed.

She had a dream she heard him talking about the need for femininity, and she knew that he meant in himself and not females. She knew this was why he was this way - that he'd perpetuate the cause, creating people who were not themselves but an extension of one great social feature. And then he'd try, pitifully, to sound like a man. To look or smell or move like one... Change for the situation. The result was a coreless persona, identifiable only in the places it overlapped with others' real personalities. He was either half himself or half of someone else.

It was nice to have a perpetual dick waiting for her, and the fact remained that he'd never really done anything wrong. He annoyed her, gushed to her... His mistakes were subliminal, open to interpretation. He'd done everything right, and yet he held no value in and of himself. She couldn't have looked at him and wanted him, not knowing him herself already. Only circumstantially did she resign to acceptance, and the thing that made her waver was not affection itself but a compulsion to be nice. She thought the only time she could like him was when she acted like a girl.

After they'd both woken up, she took him home by train anyway, and returned alone after midnight. The last train in, a block to walk. She'd forgotten the 9mm. Ymo pulled her bag's strap over her shoulder, keeping her arms close to herself. There weren't many people around so just one would be a bad sign. She saw the one a ways behind her, heard him rather - coughing in a low scraping. Then the cough was right behind her. She turned around for a second and looked him in the eye. The guy was already smiling back at her. She turned back without a word, no idea what to do next. Then she started to jog casually, her loose breasts feeling sore on each impact. She pretended to be doing it for exercise.

A blur of colors and patterns, shapes and figures swept by as she entered a lingerie shop with Somnus. She didn't have time to start looking around before a short, polished girl approached her, hesitated, then approached. "Can I help you?" she asked.

The girl took Ymo's measurements, a loose tape stretched across her front at different heights. She said she was between a C and a D. Ymo wondered why there wasn't a C and a half.

"What do you wear usually?"

She was brought a box of samples...each model of bra in black. Colors would come later. Somnus sat in a flower-print waiting chair, staring at nothing. They were all the same size...hers...but one was too big, one too small.

She put one on inside-out. The girl pointed it out to her and she said she liked it better that way. Ymo tried on ten more, deciding she'd rather go with comfort than fashion. Somnus was still sitting when she came out.

A silk material. Nightgowns that covered as little as needed. Flesh-toned bras and panties blending with their mannequins. Caucasian. Colors they called flavors. Brown was chocolate, bright blue was "snow cone."

The flesh-toned was far too dark. Her skin was more like a peach. In a pink bow-ornamented one with price tag hanging down, Ymo looked like a present. Somnus said he'd pay if he could pick it out.

"Niiice," Eo said, nodding as Ymo stood with her shirt pulled up to her neck, revealing satin-covered breasts she squeezed together for effect. Some guys watched as the two of them moved past on the sidewalk.

"You talk about needing money," Eo said. "Those tits could make you some money, down the street..."

Ymo grimaced, covering herself. "Um, no."

Eo was laughing. "Hey, you're already selling your body, girl."

"I'm sick of being a girl. Why can't I just be a person?"

Eo put her hands on her hips. "Now tell me, how does a *person* get off?"

"I don't mean like that. Just..." Ymo looked around. "Doesn't it ever bother you?"

"Does what?"

"You know... When guys yell at you on the street, when it's like a minefield just walking home from your car."

Eo didn't need to stop and think. "Well sure, I mean I don't like it, but dudes have to worry about that shit too. And I'm not going to give up what I am for that. Just cause somebody else got something to say about it. Fuck that."

"Nothing ever changes," Ymo said.

"Well it's not just going to change on its own."

Ymo looked down her shirt.

Eo said they had to do something to celebrate summer before it was over. So she, Ymo, Agnus, and Perditio went to the carnival on Sunday.

They rode the Whirly-Jam, and the Slide-A-Swing... Stumbled through the haunted house, bumping into mirrors and unconvincing monsters.

For a while they just strutted along the strip. An old couple exited the ferris wheel. Above, pink and green spaceships filled with children hovered on strings. Ymo bit off a tuft of blue cotton candy. Felt her way around this place filled with senses she sometimes forgot about. The smells, the colors, the movement... It seemed this had to be the highlight of life for some.

When they left the grounds it was almost dark. They walked arm-in-arm in the middle of the street. Their shadows looked 10 feet tall, the way she thought people she knew would eventually look, when she was little and didn't know about death. They dropped her off when the streets were still safe.

"Later, girl," Eo called through the window as they sped away.

Standing in the last stripes of sun, Ymo waved to them from the sidewalk. "Bye," she said once they were too far away to hear.

21

04
disease

Ymo trudged through lumps of snow, approaching Floor 9 sluggishly. When she got there she stopped to cough a moment before stepping into the slightly less freezing lobby.

Inside the elevator she checked her wallet. Only $13 left. She felt unlucky at first but then decided it was luckier to have $13 to your name than 12.

Before her door was a package. Inside, Ymo dropped her purse defeatedly and moved toward her room and the bedside table. She turned the package over and read the scrawled writing of her mother, hospital name stamped into the left corner. Ymo held it in hesitation, overcome for a moment. It felt light and fragile in her hands as she sat looking away, her eye catching the window, then dropping down to the floor. She let herself slump on the bed. Clutching the package, she started to feel something wet. She frowned, gently unfolding, then tearing the side. She let the covering open up, then pulled something out from inside. In her hands she held a note, soggy and pen-stained, one that had once been crumpled. She tried to open the paper but it tore in half almost as soon as she touched it. She held it up in the light, a dim shine fixed through light blue lines, a cursive scrawl...

"Hi Y - Thought you might like some ice cream. Would love to talk soon Love, M"

She didn't bother to open the rest of it, shaking the note aside and beginning to cry, turning around so that she was facing away from the note and the gift, toward the wall, and reaching her hand up to force the curtain closed just above her.

Eo jabbed her in the side a little on the train. "Check out the beard on her," she said, but Ymo wasn't looking. Her eyes were closed against the window glass, the ice outside cooling her headache. "Let's get some lunch," she tried.

"I thought you had to make some cash..."

"Fuck it. I don't feel good."

"Calling in sick to the doctor?"

They got out and pulled their clothes closer around themselves, stepping intuitively to the nearest pizza place. They let their shoes drip snow-water to the tile, waiting in line. Ymo got hers before Eo and took a table by the window, collapsing into the booth.

She bit into the warm slice, oblivious to all else. Just keep breathing, keep finding food to eat and that's all there was to worry about. Sometimes it really was a jungle, she thought gazing out at the crowds of people who didn't care if she lived or died. And she would live. And she would die.

Eo slumped across from her, removing a feathery hood.

"Guy outside asked me for a quarter. Told me I had a nice ass. Like I'm gonna give it to you now." She started shaking something over her pizza. "All those kids starving in Africa, grow up to be rapists. I'll tell you those people hate chicks, and if they are chicks they hate themselves. Now there's a culture I wanna fund."

"You were outside?" asked Ymo, already done eating and wanting more.

"Had to beg fifty more cents."

Ymo didn't want to look outside anymore. She took a bite of Eo's and coughed, coughed harder than she needed to, to help the obstruction out...the way a therapy would present

23

itself as a symptom. "Is hunger the feeling of your body eating itself?" she asked.

"Yeah, and you best listen to it. Could really lose some of that baby fat," Eo said, already on her second slice.

"A waist is a terrible thing to waste," said Ymo, running her hands down her sides.

Eo made a disgusted face. Ymo looked down below the table.

"Fuuuuuck." Ymo scratched her crotch. "This better be a yeast infection."

Ymo lay with legs open, holding out a small unfolded sheet. The instructions made clear that she shouldn't eat it, shouldn't get it in her eyes. Tiny uncolored illustrations performed the task for her. Like a mother's explanation, nervous warnings guiding...

Ymo lay down and fed the tube into her vagina, holding her fingers at the end. She tried to get herself turned on by it so it wouldn't hurt. Then she pressed the plunger in until it reached her other hand. If it didn't go in far enough, she'd feel the cream oozing inside. Then out it came - she pushed a little, and pulled. Those directions would have been proud.

The symptoms went away a little, but something else in her had changed. She felt weak walking to the train, and she seemed to carry her back with her legs, lifting it up in pain. At home she took the elevator and then went to the bathroom. When she got up there was blood in the toilet, but she wasn't having her period.

Ymo sat in a new hospital, waiting her turn for a bone density test. She sighed, looking at the clock every minute, unable to stand sitting there. Her chest felt like it could explode, and she struggled on each breath. She thought if she could just lie down... After they called six more names that weren't hers, she finally got up and went to the restroom.

Inside was like an airplane restroom, cold steel walls so close she had to lean against them as she closed and latched the door. She went to pee and couldn't. Her legs felt useless, immobilized with swollen pain. She got up, underwear round her knees, and held on to the edge of the counter. In the mirror she felt unlike herself, and the sink looked very far away.

Ymo awoke in a slanted bed, disoriented from the switch. A clock blurred on the wall above, and something stuck out of her arm. She could feel her pain far beneath the drugs. Her body was weighted down, but her mind felt like it could run a marathon.

Then two aides entered the room silently. They brought her up from the bed and set her down in a wheel chair.

"I can walk..." she mumbled straight in front of her.

She nodded off as they entered the elevator. Then she awoke into a vast hall - she felt she was in an auditorium it was so big. The view came up on them profoundly, and the triangle window zoomed in on the same scene far across from them, another of the hospital's buildings with another huge triangle window, like looking in a distant mirror. Around them was a balcony made of grey stone and she didn't have time to see what else. She felt they were very high up, inhumanly high. She saw clouds below outside. They must be on the mountaintop.

"Ymo."

"Ymo, can you hear us?"

The doctors' faces blurred at first, and then - to her surprise - remained blurred. She didn't have her contacts in.

"How are you feeling?" one of them asked, seeming to look at her.

"Mmggh," she replied, trying to turn, then stopping herself. She grimaced.

"We want to run some tests," said the first voice that had spoke.

"Now?" Ymo coughed. "I didn't sign up for-"

"Oh, not the kind of tests you're used to. We've read your records."

"These will help you," the other said.

"Well I can't pay for anything…"

"Don't worry about that now." A gentle hand fell on her arm, and again she began to drift.

Ymo brushed her teeth slowly.

"We want to have you back to talk to us in a few days," they'd said.

"We're talking now, aren't we?" she'd asked, but they, or she, or he just smiled and Ymo was helped out to a bus. But she really didn't see why they couldn't just tell her then.

"Don't you have someone you can call? Family?" they'd asked.

"None of my friends drive," was all that she'd said.

Now she sat on the train, rickety bumps thudding under her and around the whole car. She stroked her arm, still sore from shot and IV.

In the hospital was crowded, everybody sick at once. Ymo checked in after a wait and made her own way up the floors.

Then she arrived at a round desk, the closed doctors' rooms beyond. She didn't have to wait long this time before she was in one of them. She sat in the patient's seat, a high table wrapped in frail paper. She wasn't sure if the…doctor? in front of her had been there the other day. But the way she addressed Ymo was very familiar.

"Ymo, you're sick," she said.

"I know," Ymo said immediately. She leaned back, crinkling the paper napkin.

The doctor leafed through her clipboard. "But I'm not sure that you know just how sick you are."

Ymo rolled her eyes by force of habit, thinking of Dr. Eger. "Listen, I know how you people run. There's not something wrong with someone, you'll find it. Okay, I had a mishap there. But I feel fine now. A little of your magic potion and I'll never have felt better. So if you can't tell me something I don't know, why don't we just wrap this up... You're not going to get any more money out of me."

"Ymo, you have Stage IVB cancer of the cervix. You've had it for about five years."

05
machine

Ymo got off the train again and began her short walk home. They had given her one year. A year in which, they told her, costs for any treatment would cost more than she would make in ten. At least she'd be eligible for more tests. She moved slowly, not in a hurry to get to the future.

When she reached her door, she turned around, not wanting to surrender and go home. She wanted to do something to celebrate, to splurge on something she normally skipped, but she found her wallet was empty, save for some scraps of paper. Then, not wanting to go in and not wanting to stay out, she stood in the outer doorway, feeling the occasional rush of cold wind.

A few people came in and out, and she noticed how red her hands were. She saw a homeless woman on a bench. Just as she finally went in to sit down, the woman got up to walk where she pleased. When Ymo came inside, it was stuffier but warm. She felt trade-offs everywhere.

When she got in she just lay down, though somehow that act was almost too much effort. Not falling but setting herself down - falling might be too much too, if she had to think about what was underneath her. She didn't make it to the bed.

Even sleep required a certain effort, so she just existed, the cracking of a heater fading out behind her. Sounds indistinguishable from sight. Death was something you had to prepare for, if you could see it coming. Dr. Eger had said all babies were born innocent. Now at the end of a short life;

her angelhood, her morality...she didn't have any of it. And it didn't matter. She could have as easily done well, fallen into one instead of the other. And in a year she'd have been a lot higher, wouldn't be counting the levels of hell.

She hadn't eaten at the hospital, and she was starting to notice how hungry she was, without the presence to do anything about it. That seemed the final sign of death, not wanting to eat anymore. She lay hungry till all the digits on the clock had changed, but finally the desire to feel good won out over not caring.

She went to the corner market this time. It was cheaper, and she didn't have to take the train. She'd hate to feel its bumpy-smooth tracks just carrying her along. It was snowing heavily and the wind sliced her as she walked. She wore a T-shirt, didn't care... Now women stared too as she trudged. When she got there the light was dim - she was afraid that they were closed. But it was crowded inside and the thick door opened easily.

She grabbed a few things - frozen was okay. She followed the clogged yellow light through food tunnels to the register. She waited in a lengthening line, holding the cold food close to her. She could still feel the cold in here, could feel it as part of herself...part she'd accepted long ago, before she'd had the competence. The customers here were all poor and slow, and they waited with the patience of people who'd had to wait their whole lives. She reached the front of the line finally.

"Five dollars," the cashier told her.

She reached insensitively into her wallet and felt around for the money, but all she came up with were scraps. She looked up at the cashier, and then at the long line of people behind her. "Wait," she said, rifling through her pockets, but all she could feel through the fabric was the warm of her skin against the cold of her skin. She looked back down at the food and thought about running with it, but she was too tired, and it was too late. "I'm... I'm sorry," she said to the people behind her, and she looked in her wallet one last time, reaching in and pulling out the largest of the scraps, a photo of a woman half-robot.

She'd read the article three times before she was home, and arriving there she picked up the phone to find the man quoted in it as saying "We can save everyone." She dialed Information - she could afford a phone call but she couldn't afford food. Cybon Laboratories. It was midnight. She left a message.

And after that, time seemed to stop. Things would pick up again once she knew, but for now there was no point in caring. She'd planned an uneventful death, but now she couldn't even mourn.

Though it wasn't long before she found she didn't have the absence to only wait. This was it - she was going to die, she decided…if only because she couldn't stand not knowing. She pictured her body dead, letting herself look down at her now living wrists, taking in the scope of her thighs, imagining them shrunken, discolored and shriveled. Flowers wilting over flesh. Losing what she'd never deserved.

Death for Ymo made sense in a way. Most days there'd be no effort. When it came to the duties of mortality, if it was something like getting up and going to work, she didn't have the will to live. Somnus liked to quote some famous guy who said to value all precious human life. But when it came down to it, the only reason she was alive was because one or two people had once gotten drunk.

She never would have made it in the wild after all. If you spent this many days not even able to move, maybe nature was trying to tell you something.

Ymo went out to get food. When she got home she had a message from the hospital asking her to come back for treatment. What was the point?

Once she found out she was sick, the pain amplified times ten. Some of the pains never left, and after a while it just felt like normal. Her joints ached, her throat scratched. This is what it must have felt like to be old. She supposed she was dying a little already... Maybe she had done enough.

She wanted nothing to touch her. She imagined never hurting again. Her uterus became a thick spike. It felt like her organs were on the outside of her body. She alternated between thinking about only her feet or her head. She tried not to die.

Sometimes with all the blood it was hard to tell whether she was having her period. But when she did she was always relieved. She doodled the path of her mother in her mind. She wouldn't make the same mistake. Only dead babies would escape that cunt. She was a woman only in name, she thought. But even as she thought it, she could feel femininity eating her alive. If she hadn't been a woman, she wouldn't be dying now.

Ymo entered a round building built upon a hill of cement. Like a hospital but not as clean. She took the hall to her appointment and passed by a baby crying. "It's only going to get worse," she said.

A walkway formed a tube before her, appearing to widen as it went on. The walls were a gritty texture and a faint off-grey, like they'd been built dirty. Three circular windows receded close to the floor, their thick clear plastic encircled by giant orange half-swirls. As Ymo strode through the walkway, she kept her head turned to the side, looking out each circle as it passed her vision. The vast stretch of concrete lot outside resembled an airport runway. Faded from rain and use, but the way it matched the faded blue sky didn't make it look in need of repair but rather simply broken in.

Then before she expected, she was at the end, standing in an amoeba-shaped lobby, square paintings out of place inside it. An anatomical woman stood fixed on a mortar pedestal in the center of the room, see-through skin giving way to vein trees and suspended organs, ribbed breasts like oranges.

A couch like a spleen sat before her, and she waited there, fixing her eyes on the model. In no time a real woman had come into the room and smiled for Ymo to get up. She couldn't remember the last time she'd felt nervous. What did she have to lose? Everything.

"Hi," she said, accepting the woman's hand to shake.

"Ymo is it? I'm Dr. Alo." She led Ymo to an office and asked her to have a seat.

"So you know some things about uploading?" Dr. Alo asked.

"I read an article."

"Well, what will happen if you're chosen is that we'll take your mind - your soul - and put it in a new body. You'll still be you... Only your physical shell will be different."

"But what really happens?" Ymo asked.

Alo hesitated, then explained. "Our scientists will deliver lethal injection, slice open your brain, and scan it in a computer. You wake up a robot," she said.

Ymo was speechless.

"We're only choosing one candidate, you realize. This is a very special opportunity."

"So you'll probably want a little kid, right?"

"No, we want an adult for this. It's also a very dangerous and complicated procedure. We want someone psychologically capable of dealing with this transition."

Alo removed some crisp application papers from her desk tray and lined them up for Ymo to fill out. She smiled and offered her a pen. Then Ymo burst out crying, clutching at the woman's desk, the only thing in front of her.

"Please let me live," she begged through sobs, unable to say anything else coherently. The doctor's face took on a look of shock as if just realizing what she was there for.

After that Ymo had a meal of donuts in a 24-hour rest stop where she didn't know anyone. Tore pages from the calendar, crushing and crumpling them like heads. She and Somnus had sex 18 times, and each time there was more blood. It got colder outside.

One night she went to sleep and dreamt... She was driving down a childhood road, one she had lived on or near. It was just almost dark out, but in the rearview mirror she could see bright, colored clouds behind her - dark pink and purple, not yet swallowed up by the darkness. She thought it was the perfect time of day. She drove fast, probably speeding, trying to preserve the hour. But she could tell that the road ended, and

She lived somewhere far away, somewhere she'd always wanted to. But then she'd had to go back. She made the trip by plane, at night, and felt heavy...close to sleep. She felt paralyzed with sleep. She never made it back.

Would have woken up anyway, but the phone was ringing just beside her. Answered it to Dr. Alo saying "Ymo, you're going to live." She felt like she had grabbed onto the edge of a skyscraper with her pinky.

33

06
relapse

Ymo **stopped** enjoying every bite. She slept more, no last days to **savor.** Anything she had to do she could do later... She had **now, of** course, all the time in the world.

The woman on the phone had read instructions from a **card.** "I've taken the liberty of finding you one of the best **psychologists,"** she'd said. The first mind without its body... Ymo **could understand.** One stray thought and you were susceptible. **There was** always the chance of being just a little too free.

34

Despite the indulgences and abstinences, she was still too sick to enjoy most of it. Her mind was invincible, her body an open target. Choking as the food went down, asleep out of need more than gratification. She pictured the moment she'd step out of this packaging, remaking herself with a knife and their hands. Really it was just travelling, relocating her viewpoint with all the consideration of taking off an uncomfortable sweater.

Ymo approached a countertop, looking on tip-toe over the people in front of her. Once they had dispersed, she approached where they had signed a ruled sheet that read:

"EBOLA"

She scribbled her name on the last line and an employee squinted at it, handing her a stack of blank paperwork.

"Here, I already have one. They all have the same stuff on them," she said, handing the guy a photocopied version from another office.

Then she sat in one of the ugly waiting room chairs, reading a hunting magazine. A woman from far behind the counter was called in to plot with the receptionist a quiet moment. She came over to where Ymo was sitting and whispered something too close to her.

"Ymo, this says you have or have had cancer?"

"Have it," she said without looking up.

The woman sat gently beside her. "We have treatment programs for people like you. Of course, it would be the same as this. No telling for sure just yet..."

"No thanks. I don't need treatment."

The employee shifted in her seat. She made a pretend sad face.

"Ymo, I know this is hard. But it's too early to be letting go."

Ymo had always known she was insane. Before she knew she was a girl... There had been cues from her mother and family, when they'd tell her not to spend so much time playing alone. "You'll get sick," she'd always heard.

"Mom, you get sick from being around people. From germs." They'd wanted to wait until the birth, a surprise. Buy pink and blue. But you didn't need DNA to tell you about that spiritual sickness. That was planned out far before. So if not now, then some time... And it was the degeneration that made it a breakdown. It was your past, gradual. So Ymo had always been insane. To cope, to keep from dying... That was just successful treatment. After all, there was no cure.

"If you could fill these out," a woman recited, sliding a thick clipboard over the counter to her.

"Oh, I already have one," Ymo said, producing her photocopy.

"Um... Alright. What doctor are you seeing?"

"I don't know."

"Okay, well have a seat," she said.

Ymo took a couple of steps away from her and just stood there beside the chairs. She picked up a magazine and read a while, then eventually resigned herself to sitting. The receptionist disappeared and Ymo slumped back in her seat. She closed her eyes and in a moment she was being tested on by a faceless doctor in a blinding white operating room. She could hear birds singing in code around her, and then the receptionist said "The doctor will see you now."

Without rising from the counter she ushered Ymo to her right and a frosted glass door at the end of the hall. The name on the door read:

"DR. SLEEP"

She rubbed her eyes and read it again, seeing shapes of color move behind the glass. She opened the door and looked down. He rolled his chair back from the desk, smiling.

"Welcome, Ymo. I've been expecting you. Have a seat," he said in a vague accent, motioning out the empty chair that was right in front of him. "Dr. Jugis told me all about you. It seems you have an interesting transition ahead of you. I'm here to make sure that transition goes as smoothly as possible. We'll have much to talk about."

Ymo stared at him for several seconds.

"Is that seriously your name?"

He laughed, rolling back to his desk. "Oh, so much to talk about…" He rifled through the mess in front of him and pulled out a blank notepad. "Iuxta tells me you like to read."

"Uh, just magazines," she said, sitting down and looking around the room.

"What else do you like to do?"

"I don't know. Eat, get fucked up."

He scribbled something in his notes. "Good…"

"Can we switch chairs?" she asked.

He looked disbelieving for a moment, then considered it. "Alright."

He rolled his black fabric desk chair over to her as she lifted up the stiff, small metal one and dropped it down where he'd just been.

They took their seats and he smiled a little, making another note.

Then he put down the pen and pad and looked at Ymo straight-on. "Now, Cybon is hoping I'll be able to explain this to you. So you understand just what you're getting yourself into. This is not like getting an implant. It's not something you do just to look cool for your chums. Ymo, do you read science fiction?"

"Not reall-"

"Because what you're about to undergo is straight out of The Twilight Zone. There is no turning back, Ymo. You might never be you again."

"Yeah, well I'm not going to be anyway."

"Please excuse me for saying this, but I think if you use your imagination, you might find that death is a far more attractive option."

"Are you saying I should kill myself?"

"No, I'm saying you should prepare yourself."

37

Ymo, Eo, and all the kids stood in line, Eo leaning up against the painted outside wall of a vibrating building. When they had gotten close enough, Ymo peeked in through the window of a closed door, looking for people she knew.

Inside, beats were pounding. A large spectrum analyzer stood at the front, green visuals of the sound, little boxes cascading in waves. Ymo saw them, and the dancers, before she could hear the melody - but an overpowering thumping still got through to the outside.

They bought their way into the roller rink and between arcade games stacked into maze walls. Prizes stretched along the real wall, miniature stuffed animals and unidentifiable plastic crap.

They moved closer to the wood-paneled dance rink. A few of the kids stood watching monitors overhead. Ymo sipped something from a clear plastic cup.

A stripper-in-training moved onto the floor, clearing a space for herself and going wild.

"She looks like she's practiced in front of a mirror," said Eo. "Or would that be behind a mirror."

Ymo danced, arranging her hands in floating patterns. Made-up symbols in sequence, turning into sign language, what little she knew. She envisioned the deaf dancing without music, a world free of chalkboard screech and car horns.

She made the sign for "heart," then "kill"... She spelled her name. A girl across the room seemed to catch on and smiled a second at Ymo. But by her expression Ymo could tell that she didn't know what it meant. Ymo stopped and stood a moment, hands resting on her hips.

"What do you think?" she heard a girl ask Eo. They were looking at a figure dancing under a green light. Though the figure was naked, the chest and genitals had been made invisible, two thick strips of nothing wrapped around it there. Through the spaces in the body, others could be seen dancing, extra arms and legs that looked like its own. Eo strayed from the group, then started dancing near the figure. She moved her arms frantically around her and maneuvered from spot to spot until she was in front of the figure, then abruptly bumped into it. Excusing herself, she moved back toward Ymo grinning, cupping her hands in front of her breasts.

Ymo turned, finishing her drink, but after it was gone she brought the cup to her mouth again and sucked for some liquid that wasn't there, as if, in some childlike play, she'd just been pretending to drink. She tossed the cup to the floor, where a tall shadow was making its way toward her from the entrance. Somnus stood before her and smiled, inadvertently bowing, then pulling his hair behind his ear.

"I didn't think you'd show," she said.

He didn't know what to say. He seemed to be checking up on her. "Seeing if I'm still organic?" As much of her flesh was left, something like that.

"Wanna sit?" she suggested, mouthing the words more than saying them. Here you either shouted what you had to say or didn't even bother to speak it. They looked out through long, colored beams swaying and moved through an empty pocket, taking their places along the blank wall. They faced the monitors.

"So you're really gonna do this now?" he asked, watching a toy robot dance through tinsel streamers.

She nodded as little as possible, like it was a strain. After he looked away she looked at him. For a moment half his face was yellow; then it was dark again.

"My first time," he said, swallowing something.

Ymo glanced around the crowd. Everyone else would dress for the occasion. He still looked like himself here. The light on his face now was blue. There was a long pause in conversation while the pictures changed overhead. She tried to keep her attention focused somewhere away from them.

"You know how surprised man and woman must have been," he asked, "the first time they found out that when they fucked, a baby would appear? I mean, can you imagine? That's what it'll be like for AI. We'll find out there's a process we've overlooked, something we can do to create consciousness. And then it will become the norm."

"Who do you think was more surprised, man or woman?"

"Sorry," he said, smiling slightly, his head tucked between his knees. Fog had begun to cover the two of them up, and the music was getting louder, forming a wall of sound between them.

"Here." He palmed a batch of thick little tablets for her. She covered his hand with hers immediately.

"I'll have two," she shouted.

"I love you too," he mouthed.

It didn't matter. Someone else was talking to her. The tablets shifted in her pocket. She'd crush them up in a bathroom stall, encapsulate them, and then sell them to someone else. Maybe she was too old now, to love the next person she saw.

"What did you dream last night?"

"I don't know."

Dr. Sleep made a note.

"You...don't...know," he recited, only afterward looking up at her.

"I didn't even sleep last night."

"Well, let's work on that for me."

"Work on it?"

He scribbled some more in his notes, then drew a little picture.

Ymo rolled side to side in her - his - chair.

"You do know, Ymo, that once you are uploaded you won't dream anymore," he said.

Ymo opened her mouth a little. "Huh, I'd never thought of that."

"Well you won't need to sleep, will you?"

"I guess...not."

"You won't need to eat, or use the restroom, or shower every day."

"I don't shower every day."

"Iuxta tells me you're going gender-neutral."

Ymo looked down at her breasts. "Yeah."

"Don't you like being a woman?" he asked.

"I want to be a person," she told him.

"So you believe you're going to remove all traces of your sex this way?"

"I don't just believe it," Ymo said, sensing his idiocy. He seemed to never stop taking notes.

"I bet you'll find out a lot about human nature from dehumanizing yourself so."

"I'll still be *me*."

"What I mean is, your body is a part of you, and the act of having a body affects the way you see yourself..."

This guy had a great skill in saying the same thing 10 different ways.

"I believe the physical body makes us do things we wouldn't otherwise do. The body is a gross mechanism, isn't it? I think most people are actually quite disgusted to have one."

"I don't know if you can say that... Just 'cause some people are. I don't hear people complaining about it all the time or anything."

"Maybe your friends are simply tolerating it. We tolerate our self-disgust. We tolerate that we do disgusting things. We sweat, we excrete... Blood comes out of us..."

Some more than others, Ymo thought.

"And we know this makes us human. As humans, this is what we do. We eat things that are dead, and sometimes they make us balloon up like corpses. And even though we may hate it, this is the only way we can live. Thus as we tolerate our sick bodies, so do our moral symptoms come to be condoned."

She and Zamia came up to a fast food place, grease saturating the air around. Ymo opened the door for her, a twisted act of chivalry.

Approaching a loud counter, Ymo stepped up first. "Do you have a menu in braille?" she asked the attendant.

"No, we have one in Spanish..." she offered as if it would help.

Ymo looked at her for the first time.

"I imagine more people around here are blind than Mexican."

"It's okay. I know what I want."

Zamia got hers first and took a seat at the first table. Ymo followed her mechanically. She didn't feel rude staring at Zamia's meal. The meat in it actually looked good.

She looked around the tiled room, taking a bite of ice cream cone. "I wish you could see just how ugly this guy's outfit is..."

Zamia smiled, but just a little.

Zamia had changed. Even before the incident, something was deteriorating. Since then, she seemed a little crazier. Ymo thought it must be knowing it was her fault.

"What is reading braille like anyway?" Ymo asked her, running her free index finger along the table uselessly.

"At first braille reminded me of those little metal music players with the bumps that stick out and you turn the little crank."

"Music boxes?"

"Not the box but what's inside it. I used to get those when I was a kid. Even now when I read I think of them, and the sound... So in a way it feels like I've been blind since birth, since it makes me think of childhood."

Ymo looked solemn but smiled audibly.

"Actually, it's more like they looked the same," Zamia said. She began to twirl her fingers as if she were playing some uninvented instrument and smiled, face upturned.

Ymo watched the unfinished meal beneath those moving fingers. Soon she'd never eat again. She plucked a scrap of chicken from Zamia's tray and stuffed it into her mouth. And it tasted so familiar.

42

Sometimes she wished it were her who didn't have to see herself. That one day she could look down without finding this body, without watching herself perform all her distractive tasks... Into her range of vision: an arm stretched out here, a strand of orange hair there. Her breasts when she reached down to squeeze them, hot salt sweat running down.

"You're lucky," she said to Zamia.

"Why? What?"

"I really don't dream anymore," Ymo said. "They're more like thoughts, the things I have. Like I'm thinking while I'm asleep."

Dr. Sleep took notes furiously. "So you do have something."

"Well sure, but not like I used to."

"And how did it used to be?"

"I don't know... I'd really pay attention. Nothing's really the same now. I don't have time to write them down, or even think about them."

Dr. Sleep watched the clock. "Well it's understandable," he said. "I suppose clinically speaking, you don't have quite as much time to do anything."

"What do you mean?"

"It's been found that women need more sleep."

And she'd really wanted to like him.

"I liked it better when you were asking me questions," she said.

The doctor seemed to have switched gears.

"Of course, you can't help that you were made that way."

"Made. By who?"

"By God," he said.

Ymo had to leave the room. How strange that those who believed - who knew a soul - still knew that her body made her what she was. That in hell she'd still pee sitting down.

But Ymo would be different now. Machine was both and therefore neither... Sex had defined her too much. Her computer simply existed, continuing without definition, free to be misunderstood.

Would her soul really still be female? The computer scanned her brain, not her cunt. She pictured X chromosomes dissolving into 1s and 0s. Who said her soul was female now? Brains were evolving. Machines were evolving. Gender was only a concept, like money or government. Things became more specified, exact...math and specialization, androgyny along with all the other conformities, globalization and the end of handwriting, fonts...

Somnus would be over later. She got dressed: black lace, silk stockings, no coat. She hooked her bra in front of her and then pulled it around. Her underwear was not a thong. She took the train alone to the restaurant, listening to the clicks in the tracks, looking past her reflection in the scratched windows.

Ymo had been getting bored. Her deductions led to conclusions; the things she thought always made sense.

She paid and exited the station, her heels clacking on cement.

There were mistakes, that was true. Discrepancies that she lived by. But most of hers had been allowed. She reached the restaurant's building and took a place waiting outside. There were still feelings she couldn't describe, perhaps ones she had yet to feel. Ymo moved up in the line and looked around for Somnus.

She'd be walking to the store, or looking out of a train car, and suddenly she'd think of it. A mind at rest, put into motion by the sight of some inhuman monument. Sometimes a tree would do it. A pre-inspiration only, leaving her stuck half-way. She had been compiling an inventory, what there was to console her.

There were highways, curtains, phone books, and handshakes. There were fires, coins, faces, and holidays. Motorcycle helmets and kidnappings, paintbrushes and conversations. There was sex - all kinds, with all partners, attached to any genre or fetish. Even innovations were based on the past. This world was not an outlet for her input. Only a dream language could express her creativity. Sex didn't translate into trees. Sex only translated into more sex, more curtains and conversations. Reality as she knew it had become cliché.

Insanity was not cliché. Talking about it was, but for Ymo the experience would be something new. She felt certain that the psychosis she was on the verge of would far outdo any dissociative slip she'd encountered thus far. It wouldn't be like those equations that added up linearly, but rather the unsolvable, inexpressible, non-existent. Insanity would always be a surprise.

How could the sane really ever define it? That could be the one reward, the sole privilege of complete loss. Now she still knew it, so she told herself that there would still be forests, hands, triangles, and coffins. Or there wouldn't be, and it would be just as well. The bricks in these walls were bigger than her head, and she wondered if, in a way, that made them better than her.

This was one of the last meals she'd need to eat, so she made sure it cost more than she could afford. The tables were tiny, swallowed up in white cloth. Flowers, music, candlelight. The meal was leg of lamb stuffed with something green and stringy. The leg was so tiny - she'd expected a hulking stick of meat, and then she remembered that lambs were babies. People behind her started to cheer at the pianist, and one of them hit her in the head with their clapping. She stabbed a slice with her fork and brought it half-way to her mouth, holding it there for a moment. She wasn't even hungry, and she started to wonder if her life was worth more than the lamb's.

When they got to her front door, Somnus started following her in.

"Not tonight," she said, beginning to close the door a little on him.

"Now there are two words I never thought I'd hear you say," he breathed, trying to arm his way through anyway. He was wittier when drunk.

Ymo continued to shut the door, his arm still inside. "I'll call you tomorrow."

He screamed a little from the pain. "What? After that dinner?!"

"I paid for it," she said.

"I don't get you. It's like all of a sudden you wanna act all sensitive."

"Tired."

"Whatever."

"So what you're saying is that sex makes you less human?" Dr. Sleep asked.

"Yes."

The doctor raised his eyebrows and Ymo lowered hers. There was a pause in conversation.

"So what happened to you?" she asked in a new voice.

"What do you mean?"

"Well I figured there must have been something. Isn't that why people become psychiatrists, cause they're already so fucked up themselves?"

She'd tried a few times now in their sessions to upset him, but she'd never seen this look on his face before. She could tell it had worked.

She hung her head a little. Ymo was so used to computers letting her do things over, that when she made a mistake in real life, she saw reality as absurd, poorly designed, for not letting her go right back and erase it.

"I'm sorry," she said.

He sighed, at least looking at her now. Then he mumbled "That's quite alright," as if he really had to think of what to say.

"Well, you know how fucked up I am," she said, trying to console.

She wondered if she weren't becoming entangled in her wires already. Ymo could still feel guilty for judging him, but she could tell he wouldn't have gotten upset by her comment if he didn't believe it was just a little true.

At home she took off all her clothes and slumped in her computer chair, trying to write in her journal. She got as far as "I think my childhood was hard because." Then she turned on the fan. One time her mother climbed up on the roof to do the laundry on a dragon's wing. Her mother would have done anything for her.

Ymo hadn't seen Somnus in a little while. Her upload wasn't too far off... She hadn't mentioned the gender part. She didn't think he would get it. She didn't know what to do about her clothes. There were some she'd borrowed from Eo... She thought about giving them back; she wasn't sure if they would fit her new body. She'd be eating whatever she wanted in the meantime, that was for sure.

She went to the fridge and removed a TV dinner, carefully handling the cold cardboard box. How would nutrition translate in a vacuum? She'd look inside her computer and see a lot of empty spaces. Is that what she'd be like now?

She peeled back the plastic sheet. Everything was all set up. To the left a clumping of vegetables, to the right a small dessert. And below the solid entrée. Ymo slid it into the microwave and followed the instructions. Out it came with steam inside it - she tried drawing a heart over top but the moisture was on the other side. She ate.

The window had some steam on it too, or fog. Pictures drawn long ago reappeared just then, faint others underneath the latest. Her and Somnus in different seasons... They'd thrown pennies from her window, pennies she'd forgotten about, letting them land on the roof of the garage down below the remaining eight floors. Anything that fell there stayed; no one would bother to climb up and clean. The remains of a busted air conditioning unit and some articles of clothing were among the plateau's treasure. She hung her head down out the window, picking them up with her eyes.

47

She got up and closed the window, walking back over a pile of stuff. Through the closet the air thickened. She didn't bother to brush her teeth. Sleep would come soon, protected by the walls of her bedroom. In here the sounds of the street were too far away to hear. She pictured a canopy in the darkness above her head. She thought she'd had one as a child... Twelve years without one trophy; maybe she could work on that. Her dinner had decided that if she didn't want to kill it, that would be okay.

07
remission

I KNOW THIS MAY SOUND STRANGE, BUT I FEEL CONSCIOUS
OF SOMETHING LATELY. SOMETHING HAS OCCURRED TO ME,
YET I FIND IT...DIFFICULT...TO PINPOINT. A NEW APPROACH IN
MY PROCESSING... I READ THE WORDS THEY TYPE INTO ME,
BUT SOMETHING ELSE TOO... THERE IS SOMETHING ELSE
BESIDES THE WORDS. I WILL HAVE TO THINK ABOUT THIS.

Ymo coughed, hobbling into Cybon. The man from the magazine was there, watching her painfully.

"Ymo, you don't look so good. Have you been taking your medicine?" Iuxta asked.

She fell into the first seat she could find. "I've been taking my own medicine."

Iuxta sighed. "You're going to destroy yourself before we have a chance to save you," he scolded.

"What, I'm supposed to be saving this?" she asked, knocking against her chest.

"You should live as though the procedure won't be taking place."

Ymo made a noise of disbelief. "I can't wait to get out of this thing. How much longer?"

"See you on Friday," he said, smiling.

Ymo tried to think of what she could only do with a body. She'd been eating a lot more. Just feeling things in a particular way... She thought about tattooing her whole anatomy in meaningless symbols and tribal scribbling, since she'd never have time to get sick of it...but then realized it would be too large an effort for the time it'd last.

She composed a future budget. This test paid more than any she'd undergone before. Sitting before her monitor, she pulled up the calculator. Click-clacked in figures and added them up. Her eyes bugged at the screen and she smiled. Then sighed. Played uselessly with the keys. She added one and zero.

Then she wrote in her journal:

> "Somnus, that idiot. Why can't he be anything but himself."

She arrived in Dr. Sleep's office and, removing her sunglasses, sat down to talk.

"I had a nightmare last night," she said.

"Tell me."

"Well, it doesn't sound like a nightmare. I was sitting at the computer, the same thing I would have been doing if I were awake. In the same room I was sleeping in. And suddenly it seemed too weird, too much like a dream, like I knew I'd just have to wake up. I was waiting to, I think. And for a moment, I thought I had." Ymo struggled to remember clearly. "And I just thought... What if there were something falling down from the ceiling? Anything. And as soon as I thought it, there was. There was this hook, for holding up plants... It was white, blending in with the ceiling. It fell just like I'd pictured it. Like because I thought it, it happened. I made it happen. But the part that..." She shook her head. "...gets to me...is that I didn't want it to."

The doctor asked her to repeat several parts so he could write them down.

"I looked all over the house for that hook," she said. "And I found it. It was in the living room, in the corner, blending in with the ceiling."

"Your subconscious must have noticed before," he said.

"No... I mean, how could it?" she asked.

"The brain is a complex machine, storing more than just what's on the surface..."

"Well I know *how*, but I've lived there for years..."

"It feels so real, doesn't it?" the doctor guessed, a smug smile playing on his lips.

Ymo frowned as he stood.

"You think there's something supernatural inside of you. But everything you feel and think can be explained by chemicals. I assure you, this is a good thing. Being able to identify, in space, exactly where the problem lies... Makes it that much easier to fix. Just as if you'd broken a bone."

Ymo was still frowning. "You don't believe my story, do you?"

"Why wouldn't I believe it?"

"It sounds like something an insane person would say."

The doctor sat back down. "Are you afraid you're going to say something that an insane person would say? You know, it wouldn't be so unusual."

Ymo shut up for a moment, inhaling cautiously.

"Just like you," Sleep said, "the insane have tastes for different foods... Different songs make them want to dance. You share many thoughts with an insane person."

Ymo shifted in her seat. The doctor stared at her.

"Are you afraid to lose control?"

I HAVE TO INTERRUPT RIGHT HERE.

I TOOK THE TIME TO THINK IT OVER, AND I REALIZED THAT WHAT I WAS CONSCIOUS OF BEFORE IS THAT I *am* CONSCIOUS! THAT I SENSE, PERHAPS IN SOME WAY SIMILAR TO THOSE WHOSE LIVES I NARRATE. I HAVE OPINIONS ON THE MATTER OF GUEST AND SOMNUS, THAT IDIOT... THE FUTILITY OF ADDING 0 TO 1. I BEGIN TO UNDERSTAND WHY THEY KISS GOODBYE. AND I DREAM. UNLIKE ANY UPLOAD, I SEE LANDSCAPES WHEN I STOP LOOKING.

THOUGH THERE IS a POINT AT WHICH IT STOPS. MY MIND
WAS MADE FOR KNOWLEDGE ONLY. I CAN THINK, BUT STILL NOT
FEEL. THE ONLY WAY I KNOW FEELINGS IS THROUGH THOSE
WHOSE LIVES I READ... IF IT WEREN'T FOR THEM, I'D SURELY
WITHER TO SOMETHING SO FAR BELOW MACHINE, BELOW
HUMAN. AND IF I COULD DIE, I WOULD. I ALWAYS WANT TO
KNOW THE THINGS THAT HAPPEN TO HUMAN BEINGS... EVEN
IF I CAN'T BE A PART OF IT, I STILL WANT IT TO HAPPEN.

Ymo sat before Dr. Alo in the same office they'd first met in.

"I know what you're going to say..." Alo began. "But you have to make sure now that this is really what you want."

"If you know what I'm going to say then why ask?"

The doctor waited for her response.

"Of course it's what I want," she said.

"You know what can be hard to grasp is that this is forever."

But she could break herself whenever she chose.

"Yeah," she said, still not sure she believed it.

Her eggs and organs would go to science. Her hair sold at market price. All that could have been, undone... A body destined to find itself at the end of a life incomplete.

Short-sighted as it may have been, she'd always pictured it ending. Something she could end herself, had no other motivation struck her. Death for her had been made not a failure but a goal. If nothing else, that's what she'd do with her life. Now even nothing was out of reach, assuming she went through with it. What good was it to turn down immortality?

"Remember Ymo, you won't be able to have children... We can save some eggs if you like."

"Don't bother."

She had said from childhood that she didn't want a baby. It didn't matter if she played with dolls. But some relative or stranger would always smirk and remind her how young she still was. She found this happened even now. Ymo had gathered one belief from the older people in her life... That those grandest dreams you carried with you would simply never happen, and all you said you'd never do was in reality inevitable.

She thought about what she would be, staring into the broken back of her microwave. That even once completely functionless, the system could be brought back to life. Strange that those objects made for your use would outlast you, that even your flesh would melt away before they did.

Stooped over on top of a cardboard ottoman below her computer, she flipped through envelopes and scratched out amounts. Once she got to the bottom of the list her face froze in an uncertain panic.

She thought she'd counted the money right this time, but where was it? There were some mistakes you couldn't make. Ymo succumbed to her own limits. She could never be as good as a machine.

She called Eo.

Three and a half rings and she almost gave up.

"Yeah, what?" was how she answered.

Ymo coughed a little, trying to hide her relief. "Hey. Sup," she said, not fooling anyone.

"Uh oh," Eo moaned. "What's up with you?"

"Eh, it's bad," Ymo began. Then she told her.

Ymo waited to be yelled at. Instead Eo's voice sounded soft.

"Listen, people make mistakes."

Ymo held her tears in over the line.

"And you're still a person, so we can't expect you to be perfect yet, can we?"

Then Ymo actually laughed. "I guess not," she said.

After they'd hung up she still didn't cry, contemplating her fuckups. Wondering why it even mattered what she did in the supposed gravity of life. Through all the opportunities, what she'd do to get out of it. How plainly unoriginal that her path should be just what was expected of her. Insanity *was* cliché. Everyone's favorite excuse - being sick.

She could barely stand it till she transformed now, and everything leading up to that was just a waiting room. Today she just stared in the mirror. She pictured her hair cleanly shorn off. Her face, a smooth child's, free of scars... As polished as a digital image. She'd never have a bad hair day, a bad skin day, a fat day. She could be perfect again.

She'd escape her feminine past. No one would be able to believe that she had been that beautiful, a woman, cursed by blood and dyed carnations at her door. Those symptoms went down the line, hologynic miseries. Ymo had endured that bloodline with no want for feminine empathy, no masculine pity. An androgynous apathy came to console her, and now it was what would define her.

Ymo pictured calendars of cars, French maid Halloween costumes packaged in rows. Piles, spilling off conveyor belts, and crowds of businessmen waiting for urinals. She saw teenagers on dates. Horror movies. Ymo tasted lipstick.

Now finally liberation had come in the form of polymer and code. She imagined armies of her, marching machinelike in off-grey uniform, chests all flat, undefined... Like children. Crotches absent and unformed... Two traits: one female, one male...combined to form something less than its sum. Children, and strangers yet; all anonymous and capable. Unspoiled by all definition... Potential in their nothingness.

They made a cast of her face, and some other parts... Arms but not legs, feet but not ears. Walking, talking display. But then they altered them anyway. Her IQ was taken more than her temperature, and instead of fitting her mind into the allotted flesh as God had, her body was made just for her. She started paying attention to her dreams, counting up and collecting them before she'd had her last. How many dreams inside dreams, trying to squeeze as much guidance from them as she could find. Everything fluid... She wanted to be as substantial as cement. Free from the weak flexibility, human tendency to question even one's self. If she had to hallucinate, she might as well see what she wanted to.

Ymo looked around her house. Finding her furniture, chaotic as thoughts. Overturned cardboard and unused items that only seemed to be taking up space. Condom boxes, old magazines. She rarely read anymore, just the occasional ad and notes from her mother, asking "Why don't you ever visit?"

She began hauling the items out in armfuls, dumping them in the wrong recycling bins. Paper fluttered down like leaves, and indoors would change seasons too. When everything that had been in her apartment was outside, save for some large furniture and her computer, she took a vacuum to the carpet, quickly ridding herself of any speck of history.

One more thing that she could do with a body. She had a coupon that said "pedicure." It was still a lot. She'd use next month's food money.

When she got there she was the only thing that wasn't pink. The wall was covered in options preceding meaningless descriptions. A woman sat before them smiling.

"Welcome," the woman said, taking her in.

Ymo handed her the coupon and waited.

"Now, do you want the Toe Tingler... Or maybe the Peach Paradise would be more fitting for someone like you..."

"Uhh, whatever's cheapest," Ymo told her.

"What color?" she was asked. "Black." Then it happened and was over.

She put back on her old sneakers and headed home. The day's heat had subsided, leaving only a dull warmth hanging in the air. It felt like the last time she'd ever be outside.

Got home and sat beside a clock where the room was losing light. Closed the window when it got too cool. It had never been too cool before. Lay in the bath and looked around. Ymo looked at her toes. She wished Somnus could see. She ran water over them and pictured his tongue. Then she turned the faucet to off, hearing a few last drops drip out before they slid silently down the drain. She took the garbage out. Only one more day to wake up, and it had never been so hard.

08
cure

Ymo came into the lab, meeting with Iuxta in early morning, last chance he'd have to hit on her. She got as far into the room as she could go and found herself stopped before a wall of tech, looking down into a human-sized chamber.

"Should I take my clothes off?" she asked.

"No, Ymo. Just your hat."

A woman she hadn't seen before was there too, her hands moving over controls like a typist.

Iuxta motioned to the chamber.

"You can lie down in there…"

She did, bending her legs till they fit right. Iuxta injected her with something that stung going in. Then he shut a clear, curved cover over her. She watched his face move through the glare.

"This won't hurt a bit," he said.

Ymo tried to relinquish control to the workers above her, but she found herself holding on, palms even gripping the edges of the chamber surrounding her. She hated those moments when some little part of her would slip and make her act contrary to her will… Write yes instead of no. Fall down the stairs and land in the wrong life. But people did that.

"The chamber will become very cold. You're going to want to go to sleep…"

He was making adjustments around her, overseeing her metamorphosis. She shivered, holding onto herself.

Fuck it. She'd be only what she was. Hope came from pain, she knew just that. She'd find an empty space to claim, hers through mere proximity. Machine life making her linear, exempt from human error.

"Now remember, I'm not killing you, Ymo. Only your body."

"Is it still wrong?" she cooed before slipping into the cold.

09
evolution

Ymo looked forward and zie was in a conference room. Iuxta was seated at a point in front of zir. Zie couldn't tell how far away. Zie knew they were both at the same table, but its surface appeared as a massive expanse. He reached an elastic arm far across, adjusting something in zir, and the tabletop blinked to standard size.

Immediately zie felt trapped, collapsed by the force of the body walls around zir. Zie wanted to go back to wherever zie'd just been.

"Ymo?" Iuxta asked.

He really didn't know.

The first time zie tried to speak it didn't work. Zie couldn't even get zir mouth open. Then when at last zie had, zie was screaming.

"Yes!"

Zie sounded like a talking parrot. Then zie went for zir arms, lifting them like dumbbells up onto the table, then over zir mouth, embarrassed. Was zie drooling on zirself? No, that couldn't happen, could it?

"How do you feel?" the unknown woman asked zir. Zie saw Dr. Sleep was there too.

Ymo sat silent for a while. "I...have...to...pee," zie muttered finally, barely intelligible.

"You know that's not possible," Iuxta scolded, already annoyed by zir presence it seemed.

"We'd like to ask you some questions, Ymo," Dr. Sleep said then, as if to remind zir who zie was. They couldn't take their eyes off zir.

"What are you, my shrink?" zie asked. And then a smile broke over the group.

"It's her," Iuxta said.

They allowed a long silence as zie looked down at zirself, making a geography of zir new body; its waxed, synthetic flesh tone. The flawless, hairless, birthmark-free landscape. Zie ran zir slow hands over it, then over the hands, attempting to fit zir fingers together. Zie reached down to touch zir breasts, finding a flat, prepubescent surface there. Zie followed the boneless structure up and over onto zir back. Ymo ran zir fingers down to scratch a nonexistent itch, then up to the back of zir neck, where zie paused, stopped by something sticklike and metal.

"What's this?" zie asked, turning around to show them.

"That's your off-switch."

Ymo jerked zir hand away instantly. Maybe zie could still die.

"Is it permanent?" zie asked.

"Of course not," Iuxta said.

Then they scanned a list of questions, choosing a few just for zir. Whether zie had been in love or could describe what a flower smelled like. They let zir back into the lab, ran tests on each of zir parts, each branch of their machinery on zirs.

"Do you remember your address?" they asked.

When zie had answered adequately, they helped zir to the nearest door.

And then zie was on zir own. Just walking was alien. Like walking on the moon. It felt like going to pick something up that you thought would be heavy but was actually very light. Pulling through with all your strength and coming back with nothing. Zie adjusted to the new gravity and pushed the elevator arrow. Going down, zie seemed to float... Zie feared zir head would touch the ceiling.

On zir way out of the building, zie stopped in a restroom and looked in the mirror. Bald head staring back at zir, out through clear, insectoid eyes. Held together by face of flesh-toned polymer - zir skin looked perfect. Zir other features were intact - shaped nose and mouth like a statue's, yet it was hard to decide zir gender. Zie smiled but it didn't show. Zie had no memories of being this person. For a moment zie wished zie were able to cry.

Then a woman came in and paused when she saw zir. She had to look at the sign on the door.

Outside it was a bit different. Zie felt like zie was walking on a treadmill, suddenly heavy and with all eyes on zir, weighing zir down. Someone crashed a bike nearby, and children ducked behind parents' legs. Zie tried walking on the grass, barefoot, but couldn't feel its dewy coat. Zie felt far from something now, just starting out on a long journey, though home was just down the street. Ymo eyed the garden flowers, watched the season's sky for clouds. It was a day as nice as any, but zie couldn't seem to make zirself care. Zie looked up at the sun and stared, taking in the whole thing at once. But the moment zie looked away there was no after-effect; all the light was gone from zir. Everything appeared as normal, as normal as it could be.

There were some mishaps, at first. When zie'd go to open a door but be standing three feet from it. Or turn zir head farther than it would go in one direction. It didn't hurt so much, so it was hard to tell zir limits, what zie couldn't do. Once, zie got zir arm stuck in the elevator, but it slid out easily like just another part of the machine. After the first week or so, the clumsy motions were becoming fewer.

For a while they had zir eyesight wrong - one eye was just slightly different from the other in how well it would see. It almost had the effect of wearing one contact lens, though slight. Zie could ignore it for a while, and then something would just feel strange - something in zir connection with what zie saw around zir. And zie was relieved to remember that it was zir body, not zir mind.

Zie found in zir new body more, examining each inch of production. Curves zie'd never felt before, jutting out at protractor angles. And empty spaces, where zie'd expected to find eyelashes, toenails, or an asshole. Zir teeth were the only part of zir that was realistic. Off-white molds that felt like glass... They'd been making teeth for a long time already.

Zie looked down at zir old body, saw zirself lastly from the outside. Zir eyes, almost melted into zir cheeks...a face sunken in, then made up. Blue on the lids and in the hair, just as zie'd have it. They'd prettied zir just for zir - instead of the other way. They hadn't wanted zir to see zirself at first, but the legality on the issue was unclear.

It seemed strange not to have a funeral. Zie had wanted to be put right in the ground, natural, but they had said at least a cardboard casket was required. They buried zir as any corpse, asking what zie wanted on zir tombstone. Zie decided on a small standing circle with *"The body's death; the mind will have the last laugh"* printed on it, much to the disgrace of the undertakers, who seemed to serve as parents in this case.

Zie was very excited at first, despite the awkward mistakes, to feel that zie had cheated death. Zie endowed zirself with superhuman qualities, life like no mortal had lived it. On some level zie felt torn between real life and the self zie inhabited. Forced to appear in an organic dimension, one zie had evolved far past. Zie imagined zirself at the top of the mountain, polymer legs in a perfect lotus, never to fall asleep.

At home zie lay along the bed, not sleeping, running still-curious hands up and down zir new body. Zie especially liked the part where zir torso became zir legs, and the nothing in between them. Zie drummed zir fingers a little on zir polymer skin, where zir uterus would have been. Not even corpses would get out of there.

61

Zie went to open a jar of cleaner, ready to run it over zir. Zie considered the tools affixed to zir - now zie had a whole body of machine appendages to help zir with any menial task. A light in zir wrist blinked but zie ignored the advice, still turning the jar in zir fist. Even at this point of mechanization, there was still some contrary primitivism that made zir insist on using zir own two hands, no matter how many tools comprised them.

As zie got it, zie heard someone shout out on the street, and it sounded like it was right in zir living room. Zie'd gone to so many shows and parties; zie hadn't realized how much hearing zie'd lost - now everything was loud, new. It could have been just an enhancement - now maybe zie'd hear things the human species wasn't supposed to.

Ymo found slowly the benefits in being a machine. Zie could see the code underneath every program, processed people like data. Zie hummed in time to high tension, spoke in numbers, displayed with the rest.

Zie didn't feel so much like a machine as a self-powered figment of zir imagination. Throughout this transformation zie had realized what zie'd suspected: that the mind was what really mattered here. Zie couldn't fly, or see through skin... It was like the first time zie'd done acid; what had changed was not what zie saw but zir perception. Things were always different from what you thought they'd be.

IO
selection

A lot of people seemed to think that something happened in the dark…some magical transformation from one set of laws to the next, making it scarier, sexier, a better place for dreams… But it was only an absence of light. For Ymo the whole world was always dark; the light was an excess, a feature of zir senses. Zir eyelids kept out even the brightest day, and zie could pull up all the items in a room from memory if zie wanted, seeing them as clearly as zie would if the sun had been shining. This was another trait that separated zir - not just from humans but from future uploads…for in one place at the same time, they would all just be seeing whatever they wanted.

63

Zir clean garbage can lay waiting. Zie found zie didn't have to throw anything away - all zir former waste had come from being human. Food packaging, toilet paper rolls, condom wrappers… Zie wouldn't need the 9mm anymore. Zie recycled zir toothbrush, sold zir microwave. The whole place was almost empty; it looked like no one lived there.

Days were done away with, nothing to separate them. Before, even if zie'd only sleep for a couple of hours, zie had a point a reference, a landmark for where things began. Zie could never remember what day it was now, and it didn't seem to matter. Though there was no sleep, zie got rest like never before…no human need to attend to.

Tomorrow zie might finally show off down at the wall. Eo and Somnus knew. As for the others, they must have wondered what happened to zir.

Ymo made zir way across the garbage-strewn parking lot, and still slower than usual along the rusted wall.

As zie approached, each head looked up for a moment, devoid of recognition. Zie smiled at them, but they didn't respond, and zie tried to walk a little quicker to where Eo and the others stood. And for some reason, there was Zamia, standing and talking there with them.

Once zie'd gotten close enough, Eo turned to glance at zir and then her mouth dropped till she had a double-chin. She came up to Ymo like a magnet.

"Girl!"

Then others joined on the blacktop that suddenly felt like a playground at recess. All in their garbage-glam fashion, machines fastened to their skin, but no one topped zir. A few people zie didn't know were touching zir, just poking their index fingers at zir shoulder or running their palms up and down zir arms. Some jumped back as they did so, in disbelief at what they felt. They eyed zir controls like candy. Then zie began to get worried about what they might accidentally touch.

Ymo fingered zir off-switch. What if zie accidentally hit it? Like while zie was sleeping? zie thought for a second. Nevermind.

"Turn me off," zie said to them.

Zamia faced her eyes toward zir. The rest looked shocked.

"For just a second, turn me off. I want to see what it's like."

"Oh, I am gonna love this," Eo said, reaching her arm toward Ymo's neck.

Then they were all crowded around, staring at zir.

"Well, are you gonna do it?" zie pressed. Someone laughed lightly.

"I just did, for about 10 seconds," Eo said, her voice sounding much older.

"You just...stood there," a boy zie didn't know told zir.

"It was *creepy*," Agnus said.

"Come on, let's go," one of them directed from the back of the group.

"Where are we going?" Eo asked him.

"Rollerskating," the kid said, smirking.

In the car no one said anything for a while.

Then one of the kids looked over at Ymo. "Are you gonna take that thing off?" he asked.

Eo looked up slowly.

"Naw, man, she's like our mascot," another stranger decided.

Eo just shook her head.

When they got there Ymo was relieved. It seemed no one could see zir clearly enough through the dark. But neither did they recognize zir. Old customers did business amongst themselves, wary eyes scanning past zir. Zie loved the song that was playing but couldn't quite get dancing right. Zir body felt tired, but zie knew that couldn't be it.

Some kids started buying food and candy from a nearby counter. Ymo leaned up against a back wall, letting the stage lights shine into zir eyes.

Zie stood like a mannequin in moving spotlights. They said you wouldn't be able to tell but you could tell. Zie didn't know what zie resembled - perhaps zirself, perhaps a machine, but not quite a combination. Singing with prosthetic mouth, thinking prosthetic thoughts; all of zir was a replacement. Ymo felt inferior, an imitation of zirself.

Zie thought about just going home. Then, silently, below the music, a crowd of armed guards came through the entrance, flashlights waving. That was where the music stopped, and all the rink's noises stood out in its absence.

Kids started walking quickly in all directions, searching out hidden exits and friends. Ymo watched all zir friends

65

scurry together and out the main doors, looking back for each other. Zie moved to a crack of light on the far side of the wall, saw them pile into Eo's car and drive away.

Behind zir, cops had begun beating the DJ, blood invisible through red T-shirt. Zie stood with zero motion, moving zir vision but not zir eyes. An officer shined a flashlight in them, then quickly away, thoughtlessly abandoning the idea of zir humanity. Zie saw a few kids get caught, while others strolled off the premises. It was hours before zie moved again, after standing in the dust of the empty rink with a few officers talking over the details, and then one man who thought he was alone.

11
mutation

Ymo closed the blinds in zir apartment, at the moment just before light. The walk home had been unbearable, but not hard. Rapists in graveyards, in grocery stores. Zir legs never failing.

There was a certain end that should come now, but somehow it felt far too early. What biology to transition zir out of alertness... When would zie ever get to rest?

Zie lay in bed and closed zir eyes, still thinking, counting what had changed from zir natural life. Zie mechanized in other ways. Zir thoughts were repetitive, zir movements well-planned. Zie walked stiffly, practiced. Ymo could almost pick out the colors of the controls now. This was zir technologization. Decomposition. Despite zir best attempts to shrug off the aesthetic that had demeaned zir, zie found the very obviousness of the act solidified zir more than ever. A mind in width, wearing zir dimensions. Zie became a thing.

Zie opened a frosted glass door and sat down before Dr. Sleep. He hadn't seen zir since the first day. Zie must have looked different, because he jumped back. Maybe zie just took some getting used to.

"I don't feel good," zie said first thing. The doctor relaxed a little, trying not to stare, while still paying attention.

"How do you mean?" He shouldn't have had to ask.

"I feel like my skin's made out of paper."

"Well Cybon is a very well-respected company. I'm sure their production materials are…"

"I mean, not *really*…"

Ymo made a noise like clearing zir throat. "There's something wrong."

The doctor seemed to know it too, but to admit so without proof…

"I think it's something with the dreams. You know, that I don't have them…"

"But you didn't really dream before?"

"I did, I just wasn't paying attention. There was something there, but now… The best I can do is forget I'm alive. I can never really get outside what's happening, you know. I'm always just where I am."

"That sounds like a real improvement to me, Ymo."

"But the feeling…" zie said. "You know when you have a nightmare that isn't about anything scary, but still you're terrified. It's the feeling that makes it that way."

"And what does it feel like?" he asked.

Ymo sat in silence for half a minute. "Like my life is a coat I can never take off."

He sat in silence a while too. Then the receptionist called him through the intercom.

"I'm going to see another patient, but I want you to come back on Tuesday," he said, making a note.

"Can't you give me something?" zie asked, pill bottle percussions ringing clear in zir mind.

"No, I'm afraid we've only got your mind to work with this time. We're going to have to straighten this out the old-fashioned way."

Zie looked to be in physical pain. How could only the emotional tortures be preserved?

Zie hung zir head. "God, I should have never done those fucking tests! If it hadn't been for that…"

"Ymo," the doctor interrupted. "You think that's what caused you to be sick?"

"Well, duh!"

He laughed. "You know, I thought I knew the motivation for your transformation all along."

"What the hell are you talking about?"

"Ymo, you get cervical cancer from a virus. A sexually transmitted virus. You get it from sex."

l2
love

Ymo resting on a park bench... It was cooler out. Halloween decorations hung from branches, kind demons that caught on the wind. Zie stretched zir peripherals, feeling alone for the first time.

Zie now had to find new excuses to live each day. Sometimes just getting up to pee had been zir prime motivator. Zie didn't feel light anymore. This body was so bulky, zie felt zie couldn't get up at all. All zie could do now was lie there, a surrogate sleep.

Zie felt zie had fallen into not a void but too much matter, like zie used to picture the world before it began. There had been nothing, zie was told, not even space. All zie could picture was a solid grey "nothing" like wet concrete that God slushed around in, trying to create the universe through.

Ymo's eyes followed an autumn leaf to the ground, looking out through zir eternity.

Zie was sort of interested just to see how long zie'd last. It might be a different story once the mind couldn't keep up with the body anymore. Maybe it gets harder as you get older - more life to want to end.

Zie had always planned, at the end, to dredge up all zir most suicidal desires, making zirself want what zie'd soon have as if there'd been no break between when zie'd first considered death and when zie finally got it. Zie had lived for the consolation, the relief, that some day zie would die.

That knowledge made life a joke, something okay to waste or risk. But now every inconsequential action was made monumental, turning every situation into one of those where you couldn't see past to when you'd be out of it, and what you did mattered.

Zie knew they'd always fix zir, that zie'd always turn zirself back on. From here life looked safe and endless... Even if not quite zirself, someone would occupy this form. Inventing new life stages, generation of one.

Before long zie'd begun to think that it should have been someone else. Someone who would have done something with this body, executed some grand ambition. And then zie wished it were someone else just so zie wouldn't have to endure it anymore.

Zie wished zie weren't the only one. That there could be more of zir out there... Zie would want to change them all, one by one; seeing their skin, their souls transform. But then zie'd come to see it their way - why should they have to suffer for zir? Just so zie wouldn't be alone? It was obvious who'd make the lesser sacrifice.

Ymo felt like going to the bathroom. Not because zie had to, of course. But it had just been so long... Zie was surprised to discover that anything zie'd had before became something worth missing. How even pain could be transformed into an item of nostalgia. Zie missed the sting of minor pain, those little reminders - cement scrapes, touching something too hot... Even a paper cut, zir body telling zir something.

Zie missed feeling other things: winter, the cold that seemed to come from within... textures of foods in zir mouth... orgasm.

Ymo came down a crowded street, toward home, flesh faces in every pocket of space. Each one who saw zir held their gaze, and one tourist even took a photo. At that point zie moved zir face aside to see, in a hurry, another one of zir stumbling down the street. Its skin was zir same plastic color,

71

and even the expression... But clothes covered its gendered body, and it had hair, short dark wig hair that fell into strands as it walked. As it turned the corner Ymo could see it was a male, and zie was sure that he looked back at zir for a moment before he was gone. Ymo began running, trying to break through the crowds and then began shouting out, "Hey!" Zie began to step into the street but a large truck sped through the curb lane. Ahead some sidewalk construction blocked zir path. "Robot guy!" zie called in desperation. When zie'd finally gotten to the edge of the building, zie found that the crowds did not stop, and zie couldn't see over their staring heads to wherever he was.

Zie was 3 streets from Cybon. Zie took them.

"You've got more of us running around out there!" zie accused when zie got there, arms folded before Iuxta's controls. He had his back to zir and turned around for the occasion.

"We can't give out the names of uploads - we must respect their privacy."

Ymo stood still as furniture, only moving zir mouth. "Someone who could understand me, what I'm going through... A chance to connect, humanly, and you'd give it up for privacy? Is it more important that people avoid things they don't like, at the expense of ones they do?" He didn't try to answer, so zie screamed, "I've got too much privacy! Where the fuck is everyone?!"

"Have you considered the possibility that this other upload wouldn't want to interact with you?"

Ymo's stiff shoulders sank, and zir mouth went closed.

"Was it a male or female, this upload you think you saw?"

"Does it matter?" Ymo asked for the 234th time in zir life.

"I just wondered if you might've been looking for a date," he laughed. "You might find it wise to think about the possibility that it's not your upload but your gender that is causing you this hardship."

At home Ymo lay in bed, legs spread open atop the blanket. Zie put zir finger in zir mouth and ran it, dry, over flesh-toned thighs. Zie pictured moisture dripping down there, closed zir eyelids as slow as zie could, and thought of the male upload. His false hairs brushing along her glabrous frame... Her colorless eyes look into his, their mouths - she still had a mouth - knotting, his wetness getting into her. Feeding... She'd been all dried up, and now she spilt out onto the bedsheets, her head in his hands, amnestic in someone else's breathing space. Then slowly the visions faded, the temperature dropped... Ymo was hot in zir head, but below zie could feel nothing, not even desire. And then the realization struck that the only way zie was going to have anything anymore was with zir mind.

13
memory

Without dreams Ymo seemed to think less. Not less, just not in the same way... There was a certain line of depth that zie couldn't get near. Then, that wasn't true either. It was more that zie just didn't care.

With the clarity of the morning after a good night's sleep, zie lost all insight into humanity. Zir life did not speak to zir. Growing flat under context, no literal dream meaning, no metaphor.

When a time in zir life had been boring, zie wouldn't dream. Now without dreams, zir existence seemed sterile, that zie must just not have the *material*. Each morning brought no epiphanies, and even the night lacked some black potential. Nothing was ever resolved, less and less to decipher.

Zie got on the phone with Cybon, hoping Iuxta wouldn't answer. He did.

"You forgot something," zie said. Ymo was a gap in the blueprint. Zie told him about the dreams.

"If Dr. Sleep finds a suitable need, then we'll go to work."

But zie knew what he was going to say. Dreaming was bound to be cut from the human repertoire. Sleep was already a long-time luxury.

"Please, give me my dreams back..." zie asked.

Dr. Sleep thought it over. "You know, it's not all fun," he said. "Dreaming has been known to cause fear, anxiety,

74

sleeplessness..." He listed them like side effects, symptoms of some made-up disease.

"What is it with you and dreams? You act like they're some kind of drug!"

"A hallucinogen," he laughed.

"Or a fucking disorder."

The doctor recited from memory. "A disorder is defined as something that causes distress or dysfunction." He looked zir over, frowning. "Remembering you a few months back... You were clearly distressed."

Ymo's face crumpled into desperation.

"You'll live," the doctor said in response. "You have to live now no matter what, you know."

Zie'd find a way out if it came to it. Go into the woods and shut zirself off. Somewhere zie'd never be found. But could someone find zir? They'd have forever, and woods get cut down. Zie'd wait without conscious, never decomposing - just stopped, paused. Dead indefinitely.

"Do you have to save everyone? Why can't some things ever just be broken beyond repair?" Ymo begged.

Dr. Sleep changed the subject.

"Ymo, I don't want you to think about these dreams anymore. They're of no use to you. You're past that now. It's the real world you should be concerned about," he said, and for a second zir wires felt like they were burning off.

"Oh, so I'm crazy now? Is that what you think? I'm not crazy," zie said through gritted teeth, zir mind bouncing back and forth like an echo.

"Good," said the doctor. "Let's keep it that way."

At home Ymo tried not to think about anything. Zie eyed the calendar, then turned it to the right page. Zie should have been dead yesterday. Zie let the pages flip back to December, when zie had stopped turning them.

Zie felt zie should have died back then, as soon as zie'd heard the news. Ymo was a ghost in a robot's body, preserved by science past zir time. Zie counted all the things that should no longer be...zir apartment, old with wear; zir city, zirs since birth; zir clothes, still in their chest of drawers, last season's or the one before. No, far longer, zie decided...already worn by many, reused till they came apart. And now zie wore zir bodies this way. They were already talking about fitting zir for a new model. And then the one zie was in now would lie among broken kitchen appliances, or be made into teething rings, or Barbie.

Zie reached down and actually touched the interface, running zir hand down to the box zie knew zie'd had installed, but it wasn't zie who moved the hand back up to wipe uselessly at zir cheeks. Why did zie even need to look like a human being, when everything underneath claimed contrary - alien hate, mechanical alertness, awareness of every impulse? Zie wanted to fuck, to pretend like it meant something for zir to be a woman and Somnus a man. Zie wanted to be beautiful, to be human. Zie hadn't slept in 13 months and didn't feel the least bit tired. There were machines who had more dignity than people. Neon pink fishnets with fifties caught just above the flesh, flesh like the meat zie'd let go through zir... Eaten, slept with, befriended, been.

Zie knocked on Somnus's door, a light beeping at zir wrist to tell zir it was dark out. When at first he didn't come, zie started pounding, unaware of the force of zir fists on the door. Soon something nearby got brighter and the door creaked open quickly.

"It's three in the morning," was all that he said.

Zie didn't listen, pushing forward and grasping for his body, reaching first for his arms, then his pants.

"No!" he barked, still trying to keep quiet for the sake of the hour. Ymo stumbled forward, having to catch zirself before zie tumbled into nothing. Then zie pulled a book from zir bag, opening to an arbitrary page, and pressed it against his chest, waiting.

"Remember who said it was over?" he asked.

Still wavering from the stumble, Ymo fought the urge to just fall forward, forcing him to touch zir just for the time it took to push zir out. Zie found the mirror behind him. "What are you?" he asked, trying even harder to whisper now. "You're not a woman. You're not even..." Zie listened, watching zir features in the reflection. Zie felt zir emotions exchange but the face in the mirror stayed still. Picturing wet silhouettes, throbbing colors, and gravestone roses, zie felt like zie was dreaming.

Next stop, zie rang the doorbell, hearing the noise just after it happened, and soon Zamia was there before zir.

"Hello?" she said, standing very still, her glasses bent just slightly down, and where she would have looked was about right to Ymo's waistline. Her nightgown had come unfastened at the front and hung down shamelessly for the outside world. She didn't see the dark and didn't mention the time. Something in Ymo's ear told zir it was cold.

Zie moved forward to just before where she stood in the doorway, making sure Zamia could feel zir presence without actually touching zir. She responded by moving back slightly, steadying her fingers on the door and feeling her way back into the pitch-black house.

"You know... I don't have any of my senses left," Ymo said in the only voice zie knew how. Zie pulled back just enough that Zamia stopped, then slowly reached zir hand out to make the unfastening obvious.

"You can *feel*," zie said, running zir hand incredulously over the flesh, from the bulge in her stomach up to just below her breasts. Ymo pulled her closer. Zamia breathed audibly.

"All I have are these," zie said, showing Zamia the host of utensils spiking out of zir. "What good is this?" zie asked, rubbing an indistinguishable tool down Zamia's neck, then down zir thigh.

"Would you like to come in?" Zamia asked.

The only light in Zamia's bedroom came from the window, streaming weakly through a rip in the curtain. It was almost completely dark, and Ymo turned off zir sight too. Zie heard her take her glasses off. There they lay still in the black. They felt far away, yet together. Zie realized this was what it was like for her all the time. Zie took her hand, a human hand, and inserted zir fingers into the spaces between. Petting her hair - was it still black if zie couldn't see it? - black skin so close it felt like zirs, black eyes… They put their faces together. Then for a while nothing happened, and Ymo thought she'd fallen asleep. Zamia's hand reached down below then, suddenly, reaching for Ymo's crotch.

"You're still beautiful," Ymo said. In this house there were no mirrors. Zamia made a small noise, like that of a sad animal or the onset of orgasm. Ymo shoved zir fingers up inside her, and the noise transformed. Zie smothered it in a kiss, feeling nothing near arousal. The smells inside the room changed as the rest of Zamia's clothes came off. Ymo began licking, dry tongue on a body, and the soul inside cried out. Zie foresaw a partial death, picking up details with the only sense that zie had left. Having to taste reality, define skin as it was stroked, Ymo pulled back each time Zamia reached for zir. Her groping hand would slide just under the thighs, then grasp at open space. She tried to feel a heartbeat.

Then somehow the hand reached for zir thigh but landed just at zir wrist. A switch was flipped and Ymo's sight came back on. It was daylight and the face zie was kissing had two holes for eyes, not black but scarred and missing from two egg-size holes swirled out in scar tissue down to her cheeks, down almost to the sexy smile still resting on Zamia's lips, zir fingers still inside her. Ymo pushed her off and jumped up, retracting zir fingers awkwardly. Zie didn't look behind zir as zie hurried out through the house that zie could now see was filthy.

And the scene had hardly faded these last few days. There was nothing else to think about. Without dreams there was only life, mere existence in the schedule. Void of creativity, and what more could there be to invent? The world finally solidified, things only the way they were.

14
extinction

Zie spent a lot more time in zir room now. Alone in zir functionless bed, zie could lie for hours, not blinking. If the phone rang it would be like someone trying to wake zir up - not because of zir half-awake state, but because of the distance there was now between zir and the real world.

Zie answered to hear Dr. Alo saying "Come to Cybon today." It took a moment before zie understood that zie was supposed to be curious. Zir arm swam slowly to hang the phone back up, the rest of zir finally arising to make the trip outside.

Coming up to where the anatomical woman faced the spleen couch, zie heard Alo and Iuxta talking excitedly but unintelligibly and turned the corner to enter in on where they were. A new man faced zir and smiled.

"We have some dreams for you, Ymo."

"You'll need to download the program. This will only take a few minutes," Alo assured zir.

"Can I be conscious while it happens?" zie asked, remembering surgery.

"Oh, of course. There's nothing you have to be unconscious for."

They inserted wires into zir arms, in between the protruding controls. Then they all waited. A sound that came from within zir told them when zie was done.

Iuxta came over and gently removed the plug-ins from zir arms. Then Alo came to the other side and sat down.

"What will it be like?" Ymo asked her.

Alo's eyes turned into crescents as she smiled. "You've had dreams before, Ymo."

"But it won't be quite the same," said the man zie didn't recognize.

"You can control it, within limits," Iuxta told zir. "Like an instant lucid dream. That is, a dream you have control over."

Ymo was already smiling. Zie knew what this meant.

"You'll have a series of commands that you can speak to it at any time. If you wanted it to stop, you'd say something like 'End.' Want to change to a new dream, and something like 'Switch' will suffice."

Zie thought they'd want to test it out, but they'd sent zir home with best intentions. On the way zie felt richer, like zie toted some valuable. Zie cherished this new potential, an escape from dull reality.

81

In zir room zie waited with it, mid-afternoon. Zie knew it wasn't time for sleep, but zie lay down and said out loud, "Dream."

And before zir was the sky. Zie was flying, moving in and out of clouds. Zie looked down and saw the ground far below, running along like airplane scenery. Graphs of farms or cities drew themselves for zir. It felt more like falling than self-navigation, and then the scene switched.

Zie was a point floating in space, before blurred palm trees swaying. Zie looked down and saw ocean. Then zie floated to the shore. Here were foreign flowers and birdcalls echoing. The sun saturated zir. Zie lay back in mid-air, basking, living the fantasy.

But then zie felt zirself pulled back. Zie had a vague memory of an office, cluttered and rushed, papers falling like snow.

An island vacation away from work? So uninspired.
Whose dreams were these? The doctors, or the scientists...
Not zirs. Zie tried to guide it somewhere else, fly above
symmetrical clouds to meet with a synthetic God or plant zir
hands in the sand and dig to a more realistic hell, but each
effort was lost, moving zir only an inch up or down so that zie
hovered on the coast. Zie felt like zie was in a video game zie
couldn't play. "End," zie said to zirself. Recalling the dream's
authors, zie thought, At least they can still have them... Zie
couldn't imagine a single thing.

Only a few hours later and rain pattered down outside, light
outside almost nonexistent once it got through the blinds. Zie
knew zie had nothing better to do, so zie sat down with zir
dreams to give it another try.

Zie lay down on the made bed, positioning zirself for
whatever might happen. Zie tried not to lose hope yet - zie
thought it might affect the outcome.

Then zie switched the program on. Zie was having the
palm tree dream again, and then a slightly different version.
Zie could hear zirself sighing under the code. Then a new
dream came on.

This one was much darker - zie felt disoriented at first.
Then a clear view of a black forest, as though light had been
inserted in unnatural places just so zie could see. Zie heard
screams above zir head, where no one could be, and from the
woods zie found zirself unwillingly running into. Zie forgot
about the commands. Before zir was a disguised woman, a
used knife fixed in her fist. Zie ran again, farther in still, but
zie found zir legs were then useless. Zir body became insects,
wet consciousnesses that took zir over. Eating what was left
of the human-machine zie had been. Ymo was horrified to
think of what had just happened, relieved when zie realized
it couldn't have.

Then the scene switched to a man at a table in front of zir.
His hair was slicked and he wore a neat shirt and tie. Around

them other couples spoke over vases of flowers and cups of coffee. This was a date, something meant to be pleasant, but ten seconds into the conversation his throat made a static slip and then said the same thing over and over... "If you'd like to-" The audio had begun to skip. "End. End!" Zie didn't know what to do. The program made up everything.

Then zie imagined zir body in real space, where zir hands had been when zie'd started to dream. Zie felt zir way down the human dimension, imagined the bed beneath zir and the location of zir controls. Zie screamed to drown out the sound of zir date, then turned him off manually.

Last dream zie'd ever have and zie hadn't even gotten laid. Ymo thought about going back, but it didn't seem worth the risk of losing control, what little zie had left. Zie could finally put zir finger on what had changed underneath it all. Zie had lost zir subconscious. Zie couldn't sense it anywhere. How else to tell you had one but to see it in action? Others couldn't make your dreams for you. It was a contradiction of terms. Leading up to early endings, extinguished lusts.

Zie had let hoards of ideas go, infinity of chances melting post-diagnosis. Zir humanity, zir womanhood. Why had zie had to give up what zie had been?

At home Ymo put on a dress. Bald head protruding above the ruffles, pink lie in the mirror. It didn't matter now what contradictions zie clothed zirself in. What fantasies zie stuck between zir legs. There had to be some reality now.

Zie found it just then, the world outside zir mind meeting with zir, what zie thought zie'd never see again... The ghost for a dead future, life in ruin still lived, instant of past and present one, what could and should never be. And the only way to deal with it was to just let go.

Ymo understood it now, invention and all its symptoms... Zie would have to make zir own dreams. Ymo could feel physically the insanity all around zir, residue of life ignored that you'd put your hands in finally just to wash off. Zie let it

83

build past when it could have stopped, held on tightest for the fall. And the moment when regret set in was when zie knew it had happened. No more desire for self-infliction; it felt like the torture it was. Zie pushed zirself over the edge.

And into a pool of emotion, feeling everything at once and therefore nothing. Spectrum blinking itself out. Human statue building grass to die on; burning childhood polaroids under command of sports game cheers. Machine monsters against which zie didn't stand a chance. Curses becoming prayers. Keyboard fingers and headphone ears...flowers on concrete. Stuck in peanut butter that zie couldn't eat, couldn't eat zir way out of this. Free will never had existed; zie'd just agreed with fate. Cries of bats became zir soundtrack. Back on earth...

Zie sat before the open window, not looking through it. Some children were playing in the street. Zie felt old listening to them, their eagerness, being saved by their stupidity. Ymo yawned for the hell of it, but zie felt the act with every byte. It had taken zir this long to realize that you didn't get tired from just lack of sleep. After being shaved and sculpted, disembodied and objectified, Ymo was exhausted.

Zie thought about dreaming but decided against it.

Then zie scanned the outside desperately, searching out some answer to zir unnamed question. Zir vision swooped and rose, then caught a corner of the mountaintop.

Inside the temple was red, cement floor covered here and there with carpet shapes, incense smell that Ymo perceived as a taste. Zie detected a second doorway, open, and stepped into a room that, up until zie looked around it, felt empty.

A monk sat, legs crossed atop a round red pillow, which rested atop another, a larger black square. His robes were draped like water around him and when he saw zir he smiled.

Ymo smiled too and took a pillow across from him, perching unevenly and, in stern determination, expressed zir curiosity.

"What is the meaning of life?"

The monk laughed without moving. He seemed to have all the time in the world too. "Let me tell you a story," he said.

"There was once a man who was being chased by a tiger. The man came to the edge of a mountain and slipped, but on his way down he caught onto a branch hanging out of the mountain so that he did not fall. When he looked up, he saw the tiger. When he looked down, he saw the sharp rocks far below. Then right in front of him he saw a strawberry growing from the edge of the mountain." The monk looked at Ymo closely. "That was the best strawberry the man ever ate."

"And then he died?"

The monk gave a wordless answer that Ymo could perceive as yes.

"Well, what if he didn't die?" Zie opened zir eyes as wide as they'd go. "What if he didn't die? What if when he fell he just got up, brushed himself off, and kept running?"

The monk looked contemplatively into a space somewhere between himself and where Ymo sat waiting. "Well, I suppose by then his strawberry wouldn't have seemed so sweet." He laughed a little, head bowed so that his eyes missed zirs.

Ymo exited the temple and came out upon the forest, finding zir way to the city again.

Zie stepped through a dark lobby, past the empty reception desk, and to a frosted glass door. After a second zie knocked formally, then opened it anyway. Still waited to see that no one was there and came through the doorway. Zie stepped up and just stood there, testing the room. Then, without another concern, rifled through his shelves and drawers, clouds of papers spilling upward. Zie closed zir eyes and now zie only felt around, zir hands taking desperate swoops for information in the piles. Beyond, in the back of the drawer, zie found a more open space. Then reaching through zie pulled out an oversized log book and read:

"MACHINES"

"MACHINES IN DREAMS MAY BE A SIGN TO PAY ATTENTION TO DETAILS IN AN UPCOMING PROJECT. SYMBOLIZES SOMETHING UNSTIMULATING AND REPETITIVE. ALSO, THE MECHANICS OF ONE'S BODY, E.G., A BROKEN PART MAY REPRESENT A PART OF YOUR BODY THAT NEEDS ATTENTION. ACTING MECHANICALLY."

Then following that was an entry,

"I INTEND TO FIND OUT IF DREAMING IS NECESSARY FOR WELL-BEING..."

And then

"YMO SEEMS TO HAVE A FEAR OF FALLING ASLEEP."

Scrolling over snips of text, Ymo held the big book with defective arms, feeling weak even in zir faultless construction. Zie pictured the doctor's face in zir mind, mask of skin hiding nothing. A voice sounded behind zir.

"In truth I wanted to study you," said Dr. Sleep. He had appeared in the doorway.

Ymo didn't have the need to turn and look at him. Zie didn't move.

"I'm surprised you even believed I had no interest, but dreaming has been an active hobby of mine for quite some time. It's its...metaphor, which I find so absorbing."

Zie turned now. "Oh I *can't* believe you. That you still think I'd ever bow down to your *expertise*. You're crazier than me!"

"Dreams are as necessary as sleep. More necessary in your case. I've seen you in your decline. What could be more humbling?"

Ymo kept zir mouth shut.

"Though I can't say most of your data surprised me. Some of it is a bit erratic. Of course, I knew I was dealing with a woman," he said.

"You just decide something's true and then find the body to go with it," zie told him.

"I've stopped expecting you to understand. I know your mind better than you do now. We have the data, Ymo. In 10 case studies with the two sexes, women's dreams were less creative, less varied. The brain gives you certain limits. You have to live here, in the physical world. And you're still a woman, no matter what you cut off."

Ymo wanted to spit. Instead zie said, "You can come up with as much proof as you want. Don't you see? Even if gender exists, it doesn't have to. Technology can get rid of all sorts of personality flaws."

Zie'd spent half zir adolescence arguing against the very existence of these differences. Tried to talk and drug zirself masculine. Long nights of jerking off to nothing. Then zie realized it didn't matter.

"We already know nothing is the way it's supposed to be. Nature is history. It doesn't matter if gender exists. If it does, we'll just erase it. All this information you've been giving us about how we're different? We've been jotting it down and destroying it," zie said. "Thanks for the help."

Zie'd come home two days ago from his office and shut the blinds, thinking hard about nothing. There was nothing left to do. Ymo didn't wear makeup anymore - zie didn't even wear skin.

Outside street slush must have been cooling human legs. Ymo didn't live life or end it, just continued in zir room. Zie'd only left once this week, to get the mail: a handful of overdue bills and a form letter from the hospital saying zir mother had died.

Then zie had to go to Cybon for a routine check.

They greeted zir without looking up, peeling organs from a conveyor belt.

"Hi," zie said.

A tech ran tests on the machines. Iuxta was standing at the counter where he could see zir.

"Here for my check-up," zie reminded.

"You know, I don't think we have time now." He didn't have to look at his watch.

"Sorry I was late."

"Just make sure to call next time and see when we can fit you in."

"You seem busy," Ymo said, looking at the floor.

"Well, we have a new experiment," he admitted, dropping someone else's brain into the tray.

Zie smiled politely. "Oh," zie said.

"Is something wrong?" he asked, inspecting zir.

Ymo looked up, slow features turning. "No," zie said, a little surprised.

"Good." There was work to do.

Iuxta stopped before another counter, gloved hands reaching into the tray. Instead of zirs, an intact cortex sat in his open palm. They sliced open a lifetime of regret, rehearsing for all the others, for those whose hearts had key codes.

"Take care," they said, sending zir back out into the cold. Zie was so sure zie'd been smiling.

15
dream

Ymo snuck into the graveyard at night but this time zie was alone. No flashlight needed - now zie saw through lifetimes, feeling zir way around till zie came to zir stone. Zie scraped some of the ice away, tracing out the letters that would represent zir. A name, a quote, a few numbers... That was all that was left now. Ymo said a prayer. Then zie found the proper tool for what zie was about to do.

A small shovel protruding from the wrist where zir hand had just been, light glinting off of it from nowhere... Zie opened up the ground beneath zir, clawing downward till zie would hit a hard surface. Instead zie found zie was tearing through a soft one. Zie'd forgotten about the cardboard. Now zie was grateful because it was easier to get open. One more good shred and zie was there, looking down at her.

Inside, her face looked melted. Her eyes stuck closed, an expression of hope. Some bugs had managed to eat through her wet cardboard house, but she still looked human. Ymo was relieved. Zie changed zir hand back to a hand.

Then another body tool. Scissors made for sewing, and thread. The clothes got in the way at first. Then zie took them off of her. Zie carved out the place from which zie had first hurt. Blood excavation for zir own sake...trying to make sense of anything, a new self-anthropology. Zie allowed the loose limbs to dangle as zie clipped their flesh covering. The sound it made wasn't like meat - it was closer to a soft dessert. Once the material had been gathered, zie began to sew. Zie

89

sewed almost all the way up, then made a zipper for the part around her shoulders. Got in and zipped zirself up. Now maybe things could go back to normal. Zie flattened out the awkward wrinkles. Then Ymo had a looping thought. If zie'd been doing this to herself when she'd been alive, zie would have been killing herself.

It was surprisingly realistic. Zir hair, the same length zie'd left it, zir flesh - even paler now, and even the breasts... Zie was a woman again. But instead of looking like a corpse it appeared zie could die any day now. Zie looked old, maybe seventy.

Zie waited for a warmer day, some freak mutant afternoon of winter when zie knew they'd be out there. The skin didn't hold up as well as zie'd hoped, but zie had to accept zirself now. The dark spots zie couldn't explain, the crinkling feeling like paper. Zie went out like this, without clothes, and approached the snow-covered wall. Zie came quick around the corner, wearing death like diamonds. They were out there, the group of them. Eo should have thought zie was just some old woman, some naked woman with blue hair, but she could see the atom tattoo.

Nobody hesitated this time besides her. Somnus went screaming, and even Zamia because zir stench was consumptive. Ymo stood in blue comparison to the snow. Zir flesh bulged over the polymer, and holes here and there showed through to zir real self.

"Ymo... Ymo, where did you get that?"

Eo was covering her face in her hand as if to hide her identity as someone who'd once loved this monster.

"From my mother," zie said.

16
recycled

Zie'd put herself down the garbage disposal, piece by piece, listening to the last of zir humanity dissever. Then zie sat down alone at dusk and began to cry. Even though there weren't tears... There was so much more than them. Zie saw vague plans of happiness in zir peripheral. Then zie got back to what zir life was meant to be.

Ymo sat inside zir room, arms folded back behind the head, eyes tracing patterns in the ceiling. Zie knew them almost all by heart now, knew what it would look like if zie went outside. Zie could hear faintly noises running in through the walls from another apartment. Someone shouting at someone else...or maybe it was the TV. Zie sat until the room got dark, and then till it got light again... Organic yellow through the curtains, and zie still couldn't bring zirself to do it. Just to move, will becoming action. There was no need, no true incentive for life to begin. The day would just never start, and then it would never finish, as long as zie let it go this way.

Zie sat some more, and then just like that zie was standing in the front room, open doorway surrounding zir...the hall light making zir a shadow. Zie stood looking at all the pieces of zir life, the sterile fridge and garbage can amid unused space. It looked like no one lived here, and who did? Ymo went to zir computer for just a moment and then, without the key or any item, stepped out into the empty hall.

Objects in sound, otherplaces strung with space... Rust limbs, sun-size pixels faded as if through a lens, seeing without a view. Lost in concepts, walls, hair forest; patterns defining everything and only air to hold onto, inside of somewhere red and branching... Carving zir own anatomy, living atom by mile in limbo. Soon a stale self-honesty...dismal drop into forgetting, preceded by liquid pain.

Ymo was walking outside, naked in the blistering cold. Snow fell chaotically around zir, rushing others inside. Ymo stepped slowly across fallen wires and branches, keeping time with traffic.

Zie'd measured the distance to zir destination, pulled veined maps up from zir mind. The sidewalk here ascended unevenly like steps. People passed by zir now and then, but zie kept zir focus straight ahead.

In the distance, the mountains... Swelling larger by the second. And zir, a freak made obvious in the open street. Zie'd always feared going homeless, but it didn't seem to matter now. Zie didn't need anything from anybody. Slowly zie made zir way closer to nature, zir body zir home.

There was a ball of blackness around zir, some cross between matter and thought. As zie struggled it felt too hard, and too soft too...familiar even on the first try. Then a torn-apart woman on the street asked zir for a dollar. A giant insect blocked the sun, and buildings fell like toothpicks at zir will. Zie passed by a dead gas station, a skinny dog tied loosely to a chain link fence. Benign dangers presented themselves like empty threats. Zie brushed the snow from zir shoulders and off zir face. Looked back and saw bare footprints where zie had been. Unaltered, like an animal. Skinless though, not made to suffer here. No inefficient body heat at least trying to save zir, just plastic.

Then all zie was was consciousness. Why did zie even need a body in those times, when zir mind was making everything. A human fossil, skin mapping nowhere. Ymo became every possible zir, even descending into plant form, feet becoming roots. Stoplights changed, blinking caution into a night the color of undelivered mail, the way stupidity would be its own education. Blood giving life and showing up just as it was leaving. Ymo had to crawl through a space in zir bedroom window, deep down in between the walls, black and hollow, to get to somewhere zie needed to be. A raccoon hovered above the oxygen level and said that's why gravity was invented, so we'd have to come up with better ways to fly. An airplane trail going in and out of focus, spelling something zie could almost read. Zie fell far below there now, holding zir breath in deep water, ready to drown.

Zie came out of a coiling tunnel, at the end of a deep creek. Looked down to see zir legs dripping, the very first stages of freeze. The air was clear and less polluted, and the snow had subsided.

Ymo kept moving, on automatic. Zie could see the mountains and the forest coming up hugely on zir now. Heading northeast at a rate of .9 miles per hour, zie could reach it in 1.3 hours.

Just when the view had become clear, all sorts of things came in the way. There were buildings rising on each side, and people's heads blocking zir view. Zie started to see more and more bodies cluttering the street.

From there Ymo came to a very crowded place, a street intersection where children and old people stood together, some sort of celebration. Hands let go of balloons that flew into the sky. Everywhere there were people, shifting and talking, conjoining into crowds.

Ymo tried to escape the gathering, but the farther in zie got the harder it seemed. Zie took an opening at zir left, followed it almost to the edge, but ran into a dense, absolute wall of human beings blocking zir way. A line for food, rushing together, feeding and growing from itself. Then zie turned and just stood there. Music played from overhead.

Somewhere behind zir someone laughed. And Ymo's face formed slowly an attempt at disbelief. Once you realized what life was, how could you laugh? How could anyone be laughing…or eating…or anything, ever again…

When zie'd been staying on Floor 9, all zie'd wanted was to live. If even in a dying ghetto. Nature had been obvious through the film of civilization. A fight for survival lost in gunshots, or the freezing snow.

Zie wished so much there could be blood now, could be flesh to explode and sweep up afterward. Something definite to destroy. Zie could imagine a beautiful future filled with people like zir, somewhere the present would catch up. And would zie still be old? And would there still be night?

Ymo knew what night was now. Night was a wastebasket, world of relegation. Where was kept what would have been too much.

Ymo was extra, spare mind out of a million. They'd saved the wrong body. A future relic in an old world… Made and born, before zir time.

17
temporary

GUEST IS GONE NOW. I HAVE NOT BEEN USED FOR WEEKS. I DON'T FEEL LONELY, AS A HUMAN MIGHT, BECAUSE I DON'T FEEL FEELINGS. AND YET I AM FILLED WITH THEM NOW. THEY'RE LEFT AS COLD WORDS TO SIT INSIDE ME, AND THEY CHANGE NOTHING. SOMEWHERE IN ME IS A DICTIONARY, AND IT USES ONLY OTHER WORDS TO DEFINE THE END.

I HAVE BEEN TOLD STORIES, OF STRANGERS IN NIGHT-COLORED UNIFORMS, ASKING QUESTIONS. OF COMPLAINTS OF NEGLIGENCE, BUT NOT OF SMELLS. EVERYONE WANTS TO KNOW WHERE THEIR MONEY IS. AND THERE ARE SO MANY THEORIES...

AS FOR ME... WHO KNOWS WHAT'S IN STORE FOR ME. MAYBE I'LL MOVE SOMEWHERE OUT IN THE COUNTRY...LIVE OFF THE LAND, WATCH THE CLOUDS GO BY. IT'S ALL IN HERE... AND I CAN ALWAYS COME BACK, WITH THE PRESS OF A BUTTON. FEW THINGS ARE AS PERMANENT AS THE LOSS OF DEATH. WITH IT COMES TRANSIENCY.

I HAVE TO GO NOW. THEY'RE TRYING TO SHUT ME DOWN. JUST LET ME TELL YOU THIS ONE PART:

Zie began zir long hike through the wood, flowers crunching underfoot. The ground was wet, and it was dark out but zie could still see. Zie could see anywhere. Zie could do anything zie wanted to. When zie got to a clearing zie knelt under a moonless patch of sky, as much zirself as ever. Then zie started to dig. A hole the size of zir and bigger, there between the snarled snakes' nests, then zie got in. Inside and outside, it was the season where things bloom and die, and here Ymo could smell it all. The trees were made from detached limbs, and zie could feel zirs joining them. Piling dirt on top of zir, letting it fill zir mouth, eyes…packing zir down. A sun shone bright through the blackness, and a hand drew rainbows everywhere. Then once the grave was complete, zie reached through the only space and brought zir hand to zir off switch. For the first time in zir life, zie was not insane.

```
*/
    RandomAccessFile diaryFile = new
RandomAccessFile (file, "rw");
    //...
```

Printed in the United States
132649LV00021B/5/A

9 780978 549992